JULES BENNETT

WHATEVER
THE PRICE

HARLEQUIN®
entertain, enrich, inspire™

Recycling programs
for this product may
not exist in your area.

ISBN-13: 978-0-373-73194-7

WHATEVER THE PRICE

www.Harlequin.com

Printed in U.S.A.

Books by Jules Bennett

Harlequin Desire

Her Innocence, His Conquest #2081
Caught in the Spotlight #2148
Whatever the Price #2181

Silhouette Desire

Seducing the Enemy's Daughter #2004
For Business...or Marriage? #2010
From Boardroom to Wedding Bed? #2046

Other titles by this author available in ebook format.

JULES BENNETT

National bestselling author Jules Bennett's love of storytelling started when she would get in trouble as a child and would tell her parents her imaginary friends were to blame. Since then, her vivid imagination has taken her down a path she'd only dreamed of. And after twelve years of owning and working in salons, she hung up her shears to write full-time.

Jules doesn't just write Happily Ever After, she lives it. Married to her high school sweetheart, Jules and her hubby have two little girls who keep them smiling. She loves to hear from readers! Contact her at authorjules@gmail.com, visit her website, www.julesbennett.com where you can sign up for her newsletter, or send her a letter at P.O. Box 396, Minford, OH 45653. You can also follow her on Twitter and join her Facebook Fan Page.

To the people who sacrificed
to always make my life better, my mom and dad.
Love you both more than words could ever say.

One

Her eyes darted from her soon-to-be ex-husband down to the sleeping baby in his arms.

"Anthony?"

Charlotte Price stared at her estranged husband—the one man she loved with every fiber of her being, the one man she was now looking to divorce. But what he held in his arms pulled her attention even more.

Not a what…a who.

A hotshot Hollywood director, Anthony Price didn't look too comfortable with the bundle wrapped in a pink, silky blanket, a swirl of black hair dotting the top of her head.

And speaking of hair, Anthony's stood on end. The top three buttons of his royal-blue dress shirt were undone, and was that…oh, yeah, that was spit-up. The milky-white substance spread across the top of one broad shoulder, and she'd bet it had traveled down his back, as well. If she weren't so shocked she'd laugh at the irony of this entire situation.

Her husband holding a child. She'd always wanted to have a child with him…but he'd never been ready.

"Rachel's daughter," he said in a gravelly voice.

Rachel. Anthony's sister who had suddenly died in a car crash less than a week ago, leaving behind an eight-month-old little girl.

An ache spread through her as she eyed the precious child, and Charlotte opened the door to her best friend's apartment just a bit wider. "Bring her in and lay her down."

Charlotte showed him through the apartment she'd been staying in while her friend was off traveling, taking her dream vacation. Charlotte had packed only her most favorite clothes and other essentials, unsure of when she'd have a place of her own. She was getting the alone time she needed to think things through. But she kept coming to the same conclusion as far as her marriage was concerned.

Their life together was over. No matter how hard she tried, no matter how much she wanted Anthony to love her the way she deserved, it just wasn't meant to be.

And now that he was here, she couldn't help but wonder why he'd come to her. Did she dare hope he wanted to work things out now? Was he willing to try the therapist she'd suggested?

She'd moved out in June, and now nearly three months of awkward calls, not to mention the one time a month ago he'd come for a visit to talk and they'd foolishly ended up in bed, was about to come to an abrupt halt. Communication had always been a major issue in the nine years of their marriage. The sex, however, had never been a problem because most of the times they were alone, they were naked.

But talking was inevitable—over more than just his surprise bundle. She had an appointment on Friday to file for divorce.

"I'm afraid to lay her down. She cried all the way here," Anthony told her, panic lacing his voice. "I gave her a bottle and she threw up all over me, then cried some more. A three-hour car ride and she didn't fall asleep until about ten minutes ago."

More than comfortable with babies of all ages, Charlotte gently slid her hands between her husband's hard body and the soft bundle. With care she laid the baby down in an oversized armchair, tucking her back against the cushion so she couldn't move too much. Then Charlotte grabbed a velvety throw pillow and laid it beside the baby so she wouldn't roll off.

With questions mounting in her mind, Charlotte motioned for Anthony to step into the kitchen, where she could still keep an eye on the child over the wide granite bar that separated the two rooms.

"What is going on, Anthony?" she demanded in a harsh whisper as soon as he came to stand beside her.

"You have to help with Lily."

Help with Lily?

"Oh, Anthony. Oh, God." A sense of what he meant enveloped her and left her just a bit more crushed. He wasn't here because he loved her and wanted her back—he wasn't even here for sex. He was here because he couldn't take care of the baby alone. Ironic that he wanted her to play family now, when for so long he had used his career as a crutch *not* to have children.

She knew she needed to keep her distance. For so long she'd let him pull her back into a troubled marriage with suave words and material things in hopes that his attention would soon follow—only to be left heartbroken again. Obviously, their ideas of love landed on two opposite ends of the spectrum. The saddest part, though, is that she knew he loved her in his own way. He just loved making the next big blockbuster more.

But Anthony had come to her, seeking her help, and that said a lot. The man had never been vulnerable, never needed anything or anyone, and he'd never opened up or talked with her about his feelings. If he wasn't in work mode, they were naked. And she didn't know why it had taken her this long to realize that even though she loved him, she deserved better.

"I'm the next of kin," he told her, throat thick with emotion. "We're the only family she has left, Charlie."

The nickname he'd given her when they were dating in college had lost the charm it once held. She peeked into the living room at the baby just before his words registered. "Wait. What do you mean *we* are the only family?"

"We were named in the will as the guardians in case of Rachel's…death. Because she was artificially inseminated, there's no father to contest this."

Charlotte leaned against the island in the small kitchen. A baby, a husband, had always been her dream, but that was before she'd decided to end her marriage, before the maleficent tabloids and her husband destroyed her dreams and crushed her spirits. Before she'd become pregnant last year when he was away on location, filming, then miscarried that child and suffered the heartache alone. A child she'd never even told him about.

"We can't raise that baby, Anthony." She leveled her gaze at him, praying she could remain strong when all her dreams were finally within her reach. "We're separated."

"So you keep reminding me every time I call," he muttered. "Look, I'm just as scared, but we have no choice. Rachel was the only sister I knew growing up. Surely you understand."

Oh, no. She would not be swayed by him reminding her of the heartache she'd suffered when she'd lost her twin sister at the tender age of ten.

"It's not that I don't understand. You know I do." She steeled herself. "But some things just aren't possible, Anthony."

Questions whirled around in her mind. She didn't know where to start, what to do next. This couldn't be happening. Forget that she needed distance if she wanted to make any attempt at a normal life without the hurt of seeing Anthony every day. Forget that she still loved this man but couldn't live knowing she didn't rank above the next major motion picture. How could she move on if she was forced into being an instant parent?

The one thing she'd wished for their entire marriage was a baby. Be careful what you wish for.

Charlotte ran a hand through her hair, nerves getting the best of her. "Did you know we were listed as guardians? Didn't she ask you? You never mentioned anything like this to me."

Anthony shook his head. "I didn't know. We discussed years ago if either of us ever had children, we'd put the other down as guardian in the will, but I never heard a word about it since Lily was born. Children's Services can contest the will, but they don't really have a leg to stand on, considering I'm family. My background check was clean and they're overwhelmed with so many other cases. Basically, she's ours now. Or she will be after the court hearing in ninety days."

The ache in Charlotte's heart deepened with the way he mentioned Lily as his own. She would've given him that gift at any time, but his dreams and career had always taken precedence.

"What do you want me to do, Anthony?" She tilted her chin, hands on her hips, shoving the hurt and loss aside. "You can't expect me to take up playing house with you again. It won't work."

"We have no choice," he told her, glancing over to see Lily. He dropped his voice when she stirred. "The will stipulates that we are the guardians and we are listed as a married couple. The court will finalize this guardianship in ninety days. Give me ninety days. That's all I'm asking. Don't give them a reason to take her from me. Then we can decide what's best. Who knows, we may be able to work this out between us."

Charlotte didn't like being manipulated, and she certainly didn't like being forced to stick close to the man who had shattered their marriage yet still turned her on with just a glance from those sultry gray eyes.

How could she live like that? And three months? Might as well be three years. The heartache in the end would be the same.

Actually, what she hated the most was how he so willingly

dropped everything for this new family when he'd never done so for her. And it wasn't just Lily. He'd been spending more and more time lately with his biological mother.

A Hollywood actress, Olivia Dane had given Anthony up nearly forty years ago in a secret adoption. Olivia had gone on to birth two more children, one of them being Anthony's nemesis, Bronson Dane.

Charlotte had barely caught her breath from being shunted aside for his new family and now he was adding another layer to her hurt. Dangling this promise of a family in front of her as if they would all live happily ever after. Considering her upbringing and the tragic death of her sister, she knew better.

"This won't work, Anthony," she repeated, fear gripping her heart. "I can't live with you again, not for any amount of time. I'm trying to move forward and I can't do that if I'm getting pulled back into the life that left me shattered."

She hadn't meant to voice her thoughts out loud, but now she had, she wasn't sorry. He needed to know what he'd done to her, how his actions and selfishness had chiseled away their marriage slowly, but most definitely surely. A bit of relief swept over her now at finally telling him how she felt. Not that her declaration would change anything. No matter her physical attraction, she had to guard her heart.

"I know you're hurt, and I'm not trying to make this harder on you, but Lily needs a woman in her life," he pleaded. "I need my wife. I've called the designer and she turned one of the spare rooms into a nursery when I went up to San Jose to get Lily yesterday. She should be finishing up today. She put three people on the project and since the room only needed furniture changed and some paint, we should be good to go once we get home."

Charlotte sighed and glanced at the precious bundle who had no idea of the turmoil her life was in. Charlotte's heart was not ready for another beating, but she knew what she needed to do for the welfare of this innocent child. Security for Lily had to take precedence over anything else. Especially over her jumbled feelings for her husband.

"Fine. You have ninety days." Charlotte looked her husband dead in the eye—those same eyes that she'd fallen in love with. She'd hold off on speaking with her attorney until the guardianship was legal. "Lily's needs must come first. But I'm not moving back into our bedroom. I'll take the spare room on the other side of her."

Anthony clenched his jaw. "You're not going to even try with me during this time? Why not share our room? Let me show you I can be the husband you want me to be."

"You had nine years of marriage, Anthony. You can't decide to try now just because I'm convenient." Charlotte lifted her chin and crossed her arms over her chest to prevent hurt from seeping back in. "And you can't expect me to jump back into your bed. I'm moving back in for Lily and only Lily."

Anthony studied Charlotte and her defensive, defiant stance. She was going to make this hard, but that's nothing less than he deserved. After all the years she'd stood by him, even when he'd pushed her needs aside, he deserved all the anger and hatred she threw at him. That didn't stop him from wanting her, though.

But she was moving back in, so he'd take that small victory and work with it. Soon, he vowed, she'd be back in their master bedroom, where she belonged. No matter the distance or hurt between them, Anthony couldn't deny the way his wife turned him on with just a glance or a smile.

Too bad sex couldn't fix all the problems in a marriage. They'd been hot for each other from day one when they'd met at a college party. Even though they hadn't married until many years later, the passion never fizzled. Obviously, considering he'd come to talk to her a month ago and they never got around to having a conversation.

Anthony swallowed the lump of guilt for being the driving wedge in their separation. There was no denying that, but having his wife walk out was one hell of a wake-up call. He had a feeling she'd contacted her lawyer, but he didn't know for sure. All he could hope for was to show her he was ready to be the man he needed to be in order to keep her where she belonged. By his side.

"I understand," he told her. "But that doesn't mean I won't stop fighting for you and this family we've been given."

Charlotte's sad smile made his chest tighten. "This changes nothing, Anthony. And now you're ready to step up for this child, it breaks my heart even more because I wanted for so long to have a baby with you. So I'm staying for Lily. Not you."

Anthony knew his wife had a breaking point, and he knew in these upcoming ninety days he'd probably reach it. "We need to at least put up a united front until we can see where to go from here. And I don't think ninety days is too much to ask. Give me a chance, too, Charlie. I need you, and Lily's just had her mother taken from her and needs that motherly bond."

Anthony tamped down the hurt of losing his sister. He couldn't fall apart. Not now when his life was at stake and Lily needed him to be strong. The stable ground he'd stood on for so long was crumbling beneath him and he'd be damned if he wouldn't fight with everything he had.

He could mourn for his sister later, in private. Right now he needed to get his family back on track. Lily may be an unexpected issue, but she was also a blessing and a silver lining. He'd almost lost Charlotte to his selfishness and now that he was given another chance, he planned on winning her back.

God help them all. Babies certainly weren't his strong suit and since he was being honest with himself, babies terrified him.

Charlotte's eyes misted. "I can't replace her mother. No one can."

"I'm not asking you to replace her," Anthony replied, stepping forward and taking Charlotte's hands in his. "I'm asking you to love her and care for her. I'm asking you to just keep an open mind as far as we are concerned. I never wanted to lose you, Charlotte. Never."

Charlotte's lids fluttered, sending one lone tear sliding down her porcelain skin. She looked back up into his eyes, determination overriding the sadness. "I'm only moving in under certain conditions."

Conditions he could live with. Conditions he could break through—and get her back where he wanted her. In his bed, *their* bed, and in his life forever.

"Name them."

She stepped back, breaking their brief contact. "I won't sleep in your bed. Ever."

That one was too easy. He knew just how to manipulate her when it came to seduction. Knew where to touch, what to say. Best not to mention that and just let her think things were in her control—as any good husband would. Too bad he'd learned that lesson so late.

"Okay. What else?"

"This is only temporary until we can work on a custody arrangement. Once the ninety days is up and the court approves the guardianship, our lawyers will draw up a mutually agreeable plan."

So she had talked to her attorney. No matter. Three months was plenty of time for him to win her back. "Fine."

"This baby and our living arrangement changes nothing between you and me. Lily has to be top priority now. Are we clear?"

His eyes roamed over her body, a mental image of her curled beside him in their bed making him smile as he leveled her gaze.

"Crystal."

Two

"Welcome back, Mrs. Price."

Charlotte cringed, but smiled at Monique, the maid who'd been with them for nearly five years. "I'm not actually back, but thanks."

Monique nodded with a grin and continued her cleaning regimen in the formal living room. The very room where Charlotte had hosted numerous parties for the hardworking employees of the Children's Hospital. Those parties always took place when Anthony was out of town. Supporting the hospital filled a huge void in her life, her heart.

At the start of Anthony's career, she'd been so proud of his work, his talent, and she'd attended every premiere and awards ceremony, no matter how small. But when his dreams became his sole focus and she became nearly invisible in their marriage, Charlotte resigned herself to the fact that her dreams were never going to come true. So she'd started staying behind the scenes and throwing herself into her volunteer work at the Children's Hospital.

Charlotte pulled a sleeping Lily tighter against her chest, refusing to be drawn back into a world she needed to say good-bye to. Every room held so many memories—both good and bad. The past several years played over in her head like a silent movie.

Hating all the emotions swirling around over being home, Charlotte focused on the sweet-smelling baby in her arms and moved forward into her home.

No, she couldn't think of this place as home, not if she wanted to hold on to the small hope that she would be fine in her new life without Anthony once all this was over. But how could she move forward if she still considered this her home? She'd never make it through the next few months if she didn't keep the mind-set that this was temporary, only until the court approved the guardianship and they could work out a custody arrangement. She knew he wanted to try to salvage their relationship, but she highly doubted he'd be able to put forth the effort a strong marriage required. He certainly hadn't done so before, so why should this be any different?

Charlotte sighed, taking in the beautiful, open foyer with curved staircase and marble pillars separating the living area. Just this morning she'd been house-sitting in her best friend's condo, evaluating how she could move on fast and far without the pain following. But now she was back and the pain sliced even more deeply.

"I'll have your stuff put into the room with the balcony overlooking the pool, as you requested," Anthony told her as he led her upstairs.

Charlotte moved up the grand staircase that she'd loved since they'd moved in. A large, crystal chandelier descended from swirling artwork on the high ceiling, sending a kaleidoscope of colors all over the marble floor in the center of the staircase.

"I'm surprised you agreed so easily to my being in a separate room," she told him as they reached the landing.

He took her elbow, turning her to face him. Those mesmerizing eyes bore into hers, making her heart skip a beat. "While I respect your wishes, I should warn you. I won't stop trying to win you back. I'll never give up."

Fear washed over her. Not fear of him. Fear of herself and what would come in their time together. How could she resist him on a physical level? She'd never been able to, and it had been a month since she'd touched him—a rare occurrence for them.

But she had to have some willpower, some self-control in order to make Lily's life strong and stable.

Stable was something she deserved, too. But the welfare of the baby came first. And hopefully, if she could focus solely on the innocent baby, maybe she wouldn't have to deal with how just one look, one brief touch from Anthony still had her tingling inside.

Charlotte moved down the wide hallway, breaking free of Anthony's strong grasp. She walked into the room where the designer had quickly transformed a guest room into a nursery. The pale pink walls made the new white furniture and crisp eyelet curtains pop with a fresh, calming ambience. A lump of sorrow consumed her. This was the room she'd always hoped would be a nursery for their child. The size was perfect and the crib by the window would let in the morning sun, welcoming any child to a new day.

It was one year ago she'd miscarried, and holding on to Lily brought all of those painful memories to the surface.

Charlotte stared down at the baby as tears gathered in her eyes. The thought that Rachel would never see Lily take her first steps, never see her off to school or marry one day really hit home. Charlotte had wanted all those things and more with the baby she'd lost. But fate had brought her and Lily together for a reason.

"You okay?"

Anthony moved in behind her, placing a warm hand on

the small of her back. It would be so easy to lean on him right now, but where would that get her? For now she was alone with her emotions.

"It's just a lot to take in," she whispered. "Being back here, Lily, Rachel's death."

"I know."

His voice, thick with his own emotion, pulled at her. She'd never once, in all their nine years of marriage, seen him show this kind of emotion. Other than expressing his love for her, he'd never opened up, shown her anything deeper that would make him appear vulnerable. Anthony Price was too proud, too strong to let anyone, including his wife, think he was less than perfect at all times.

Like the time his world was flipped upside down nearly a year ago when he'd discovered the truth about his adoption. He'd been thrown into a family just as famous as he, and he hadn't sought her out for guidance, comfort or even to talk. He'd shut her down once again and slid just one more thing between the two of them, sending her back one more slot on his priority list.

And then his sister had died. Now was not the time to go into all the reasons working on this marriage was a bad idea.

"I'm sorry about Rachel." She turned, looked at him through teary eyes. "I'm sorry I wasn't there for the funeral, but I just... I couldn't be."

Anthony nodded. "I understand. It's more important that you're here now. For Lily."

For Lily? Charlotte doubted that was the main reason he wanted her here, but helping with the baby was all he was getting from her. Her heart couldn't afford any more emotional beatings.

"She sleeps a lot." Anthony smiled down at his niece. "Is that normal?"

"For her age it is. They generally nap about twice a day, so she's fine. Her world has been disrupted and I'm sure she's noticed that things aren't the same. We just have to try to keep her life on some type of regular schedule. That's best for babies."

"You're good for her," Anthony said, looking back up into her eyes. "And me."

No comment was necessary. What could she say? A baby didn't change a thing. He'd warned her that he would try to get her back during these next few months, which meant she had to totally steel herself against his charms. And since she'd been married to him for the past nine years, she pretty much knew every angle he would work.

Charlotte took in the room's soft, delicate toile decor and laid Lily in her sleigh crib. The chandelier mobile overhead would be a beautiful sight for her to wake up to. Charlotte only hoped the child got used to the strange surroundings and adjusted quickly.

She also hadn't missed the fact that one of her paintings of little girls playing in a field hung just over the rocking chair. She wondered if Anthony had asked the designers to hang the piece that had been in another spare bedroom.

Turning toward Anthony, she put a finger to her lips for him to be quiet and slipped from the room. Once in the hallway, she smiled. "The room is gorgeous. Did you use Hannah again?"

"Who else? I hope you don't mind I moved the painting. I told her you would want it in there."

Charlotte couldn't help the "aww" moment that just moved through her. That warmth of such a simple gesture had her wishing their welcoming a baby into the house was under different circumstances.

Anthony moved down the hall toward the master suite. "Come in here so we can talk."

Charlotte balked at his commanding tone. For once couldn't the man ask something? Everything was always on his terms, his way.

Nonetheless, she entered the room they'd shared for years, the room they'd made love in countless times. Her body responded, but she tamped down any desire she had. She could not give in to Anthony, no matter how much she missed his touch.

Her eyes darted to the canopy bed with gold sheers that draped and puddled on the white carpet around the four-poster. He hadn't changed a thing in the three months since she'd been gone. Even their wedding picture still sat on the bedside table… on his side of the bed. She couldn't help but wonder what he thought when he looked at it.

Charlotte stared at the young couple—a dashing groom and a glowing bride. Recognition was scarce, though. That couple didn't exist anymore and Charlotte almost wanted to go back and have a do-over—knowing what she did now. Maybe if she'd been more forthright about her feelings, made Anthony open up about everything he kept bottled inside, they wouldn't be in the midst of an inevitable divorce.

But only in movies did people have that second scene to get things right.

Everything in her heart, her soul, wished they'd gotten it right the first time around. She couldn't turn off her love, but maybe in time she could learn to live with that ever-pressing weight on her shattered heart.

"Tell me you don't feel anything being here with me," Anthony whispered, moving close to her. "I know you feel the same thing I do when we step into this room. We've never been able to keep our hands off each other and now is no exception."

Charlotte held up a hand, because God help her if he touched her, all her resolve would go out the window and she needed to be strong. For once she was going to put herself first.

"What I feel, or what you feel, for that matter, is irrelevant. The problem is your affair with your career, never opening up to me and always assuming money will buy happiness… mainly mine."

"You seemed happy for a long time, Charlotte. I honestly don't know what changed and why you distanced yourself."

His eyes roamed over her face, to her lips then back to her eyes. "Besides, that money is what has helped you with your children's charity."

So he had no clue why she'd started distancing herself. That proved all the more how self-absorbed he'd been.

"My charity was built up with donations, fundraisers and a lot of hard work," she retorted.

"Yes, but it was the Price name that got you where you are."

Fury bubbled within her. "Are you insinuating that I couldn't have done this on my own?"

Anthony tucked his hands in his pockets. "Not at all. I'm merely telling you that your name and status in this town drew a different crowd."

No way was she letting him take credit for the good work she had done over the years. "I don't care who donated. I'm just thankful to get enough money for the new children's wing they're adding to the hospital."

The thought that another unit was needed to aid sick kids made everything else in her life pale in comparison. There were so many ill children and here she was feeling sorry for herself for moving back into her Hollywood Hills mansion. Something was definitely wrong with this picture.

"You're going to have to slow down, you know."

Charlotte focused back on Anthony. She braced her hands on her hips, tilting her head. "Slow down with what?"

"Your volunteer work. With having Lily, your time is going to be limited. I'll have to cut back, as well."

Charlotte laughed. "I'm not handicapped, Anthony. Millions of women work and care for their family. I'm certainly not cutting back when I've worked so hard to see this wing built. The dedication is in a few months and I plan on seeing this through."

"And once it's done, then what?" he asked, crossing his arms over his broad chest. "I know this is important to you, but—"

"But nothing." A helpless laugh escaped her. "I will take

care of Lily just fine. I want her to grow up learning to help others and that not everything needs to be done in order to get a paycheck."

"That paycheck has given you a home, a life that you never would've had otherwise."

Charlotte turned her back, unable to look him in the eye. "I never asked for any of this, Anthony. Never. All I wanted was a happy marriage, a family."

"I'm giving you a family now," he said, placing a hand on her shoulder and squeezing gently. His familiar crisp scent surrounded her. "I know how much children mean to you. I know I wasn't putting you first. But I'm ready now."

How many times had she longed to hear him say that? To know that her needs and wants matched his. If only they'd discussed these big milestones before saying "I do," but they'd been young and in love and at the time, that's all that mattered. He was offering security and a home of love…two things she'd never had.

She turned back to face him. Years of heartache and lack of communication settled between them. "I don't want a family out of guilt or obligation. I wanted a family out of love. I will take care of Lily like she's my own, but know that we won't be raising her together."

"Don't shut me out," he whispered. "Don't. You supported me once, even enjoyed my work. I know we've changed over the years, but I never stopped loving you. Surely the lies from the tabloids…"

Charlotte shook her head. "No, I know you'd never cheat on me. You never could find time for me, let alone someone else. That was the problem, Anthony. You're so self-absorbed, you can't see I would've done anything for you. And for years… I did."

His eyes bored into her, the muscle in his jaw clenched. "I won't lose you. I won't."

His mouth came down on hers, and the force of his hold

trapped her hands between their bodies. Charlotte clutched his shirt, whether to shove him back or hold on for stability she had no clue. No one could make her nerves and hormones spike like Anthony. No one could match his passion and intensity.

And no one else could elicit both love and hate in her at the exact same time.

But she couldn't afford to let sex cloud her view of reality, and the reality was that Anthony would never put anything or anyone above his star-studded career.

Charlotte pulled back, staring into his mesmerizing eyes, knowing how fast and easy she could lose herself in them. "Don't. Don't touch me like you have the right. I've said it before, but obviously it bears repeating. Nothing's changed."

Anthony's hand cupped her cheek. "Everything's changed, Charlie, and the sooner you realize I'm not giving up, the easier this transition will go."

Anthony sat in his study looking over his sister's will. What in the hell had she been thinking not telling him about the guardianship in the event of her death?

Probably what most people thought when making a will— they wouldn't die young so there was no need to worry.

But damn, this was something he needed to know in advance, instead of being dealt another blow so soon after her death.

Rachel's death.

Those two words had been bouncing around his head and his heart for days. His beautiful, vibrant sister was gone. He'd never see her smile again unless he looked at old pictures. Baby Lily would never see just how much her mother loved her. So much so that she'd been artificially inseminated because she hadn't been looking for a relationship and had wanted a child.

How could fate be this cruel to have his sister taken away, his wife on the verge of divorcing him and the discovery that he was the biological son of Hollywood's most recognized star all in the span of a year? His life had taken a dramatic twist, and he honest-to-God didn't know which way was up anymore.

This time last year his world had upended when he'd discovered he had been given up for adoption at birth by the Hollywood icon Olivia Dane. Not only that, he'd discovered his most hated rival, Bronson Dane, was his half brother. Unfortunately, with Bronson as Hollywood's top producer and Anthony one of the top directors, their paths crossed.

Since the truth had come out, tabloids had exploited the family's forty-year-old secret. The four of them—his biological mother and siblings Bronson and Victoria—had all put up a united front and issued a press release, but no public appearances had been made together. Anthony hadn't had time to take a break between work and fielding media inquiries. His assistant deserved a raise for all the calls and emails she'd had to answer.

Anthony's eyes drifted back down to the document stating that he and Charlotte were guardians of Lily. A knot formed in his stomach. His knowledge of babies was very limited. All he knew, as of this moment, was that Charlotte had no problem putting Lily to sleep and all his niece did when he held her was scream and cry.

He had no clue how to make a bottle, though he'd winged it the past couple days when no one else had been around. The diaper thing was still very iffy, and he wasn't sure if he was supposed to use that half container of wipes when her diaper had nearly exploded, but he wanted to be safe. He had a master's degree, for crying out loud, and had worked on multimillion-dollar movie sets, so why did some powder formula and moist wipes terrify him?

Because this was his sister's kid. Because he would do everything in his power to honor his sister's memory and love and care for this child like his own. And because he wanted to prove to Charlotte he could do family and a career.

Family was starting to mean more and more to him. He and

his sister had really banded together after their parents had passed away—his father from a heart attack and his mother after a long battle with thyroid cancer.

And when he'd discovered who his birth mother was, Rachel had urged him to contact her, to make a relationship and try to put the differences with Bronson aside. With the unsettled atmosphere surrounding his marriage, he'd found it easier to open up to his sister. Just one more of the communication mistakes he'd made.

And even though Rachel had been his best friend, he never told her about his marital problems. She'd read the tabloids, seen the damning headlines, but he'd always been able to convince her the media was just fishing for a story. No way would he admit defeat to anyone, even to himself. Especially to himself.

The marriage was not over. He'd do everything in his power to show Charlotte he was the husband, the father she wanted him to be.

No, children weren't something he'd been willing to negotiate before while working, but now everything had changed. Fate had handed him a second chance at a family and he was grabbing hold with both hands, never letting go.

Anthony calculated the time in his head. Ninety days to convince Charlotte they were meant to be, now more than ever. Ninety days to stay by her side and bond with his niece.

Ninety days to have her fall in love with him all over again and win her back, using every means necessary.

And he knew just where to start.

Three

"What are you doing?"

Anthony cringed at the tone in Charlotte's voice. "Packing."

Without turning to look at her, he continued gathering his things and folding them into his suitcase. He knew this would get ugly, but there was no way to avoid the confrontation. He hadn't told her he needed to be away on business. Had he mentioned it before he got her to move back in, she never would've come.

All he had to do was get through these next two days and he'd be back home where he could prove to her just how willing he was to win her over. Their time together would be rough, but he was more than ready to face this obstacle. After all, he'd been the root of her problem.

"Typical." Charlotte moved into the room, stood at the end of the bed they'd once shared and crossed her arms over her chest. "I've been back less than twenty-four hours and you're already running off. So much for the ninety days you asked for."

With a sigh, Anthony fisted his boxers and turned to face her. "I'm hosting the Emmy Awards. There was no getting out of this. I'll fly home straight after, so you'll only be here with Lily for two days. Tops. I've already told the staff to get you anything you need and to make sure you're doing okay."

"I don't need to be watched over. I need my husband to make good on his promise." She ran a hand down her sleek blond hair and sighed. "Honestly, I expected no less than for you to return to business as usual. But I'd hoped you'd make an exception with Lily here now."

"Charlie—"

"No." She held a hand up. "I'm not picking a fight. I'm here for Lily. Do what you have to, but know that if you can't put her needs first, you will miss something beautiful in your life."

He didn't get a chance to add that he'd already lost out on the beauty in his life when she'd moved out three months ago. But just as quickly as she'd come in, she was gone, leaving him feeling just as he should…unworthy. He was nearly forty years old and all he had to show for his life were some Oscars on his bookshelves, numerous blockbuster films and a broken marriage. Had all the recognition and countless awards over the years been worth everything he'd sacrificed?

Dammit. Hindsight was hell on your conscience.

He'd known Charlotte would be hurt by his swift departure right after she'd moved back in, and had expected her to be angry, but he hadn't anticipated her to give up without an argument. Not that he wanted to argue, but he was ready for it, had even rehearsed his speech. But he had to admit that her thinking so little of him hurt more than he thought it would. Her harsh words and cold stares, though, were nothing less than he deserved.

Her reaction, or lack thereof, slapped a dose of reality in his face. Obviously, he'd been a selfish bastard to her for a while and it took losing his wife and his sister, and gaining guardianship of his niece, for him to really wake up. Shame consumed him at the man he'd become, a man he barely recognized.

And now he was left holding his boxers, staring at the spot Charlotte had just vacated. Was she really just here for Lily? Could she turn off her feelings for him so easily? Did she have no intention at all of fighting for them? After all the time she'd begged him to go to counseling, he gave in and went…once. After all the years she'd told him she needed him to be around more, to be more attentive to her needs. True, he deserved no less. He certainly didn't deserve her dedication or love, but he still needed her more than he ever could've imagined.

Well, she may be done, but he wasn't. He refused to see that this marriage was coming to a close. This was his first attempt at juggling work and family now that he was making a conscious effort. Once he returned from his trip, he had a little surprise for his girls.

His girls.

Anthony smiled as he tossed in the last of his items and zipped his suitcase. He had two amazing females in his life and there was no way he was going to screw that up. Yes, Charlotte may be angry and hurt with him now, but once he arrived back home, she'd see just how committed he was to their new family.

New family seemed to be the theme for his life lately. Between the Danes and Lily, he'd taken on a whole new set of loved ones. He hoped Charlotte would go with him on this journey that was taking him from the only family he'd known into uncharted territory. Charlotte was his rock, the strongest point in his life. She was familiar and he needed her to hold on to during this life-altering time. She mattered more than anyone and he had to make her see that. He'd failed miserably in the past, but she was worth fighting for, and he wouldn't stop now, just because things were getting difficult.

He'd turned his back on her during their marriage and just when she'd laid down the ultimatum of her or his career, he'd discovered his biological mother and siblings, ignoring her once again in favor of others.

With Rachel's death so fresh, he needed Charlotte now more than ever to understand that he wasn't pushing her aside, he needed her to stand by his.

He'd never, ever meant to hurt her and he knew this was only the beginning of a very long, very emotional process for both of them. And, yes, he was going down this path to fight for the marriage he was so desperately clinging to and he was going to drag her along with him. Because he was not giving up. It may have taken a year of life-altering changes and Charlotte leaving to open his eyes, but now that he saw exactly what he stood to lose, he couldn't move forward happily in his life without her.

If he didn't have Charlotte, no amount of family he connected with or films he made could fill that void.

She'd counted on his leaving, counted on his turning back to his old ways. But one thing she may not be counting on, the one thing that would keep this marriage together, was the fact he loved her more than anything. He would fight for her with everything in him. And it was time to stand up and be the man, husband and now father she needed and expected him to be.

With a warm bedtime bottle, Charlotte settled onto the damask sofa in her bedroom, cradling Lily in her arms. All the while keeping her eyes on the television, which just so happened to be tuned to the channel where the Emmy Awards were being telecast. Could she help it if that's what popped up when she switched on the TV? She'd barely spoken to Anthony since he'd left yesterday morning, but she'd watched him since he'd come onto the screen.

"I'm not watching for me," she told Lily as she slid the bottle between her puckered lips. "I wanted you to see your uncle Anthony on TV. It's so rare for him to be in front of the camera."

When he walked across the lighted stage wearing a black

suit with a charcoal-gray shirt and matching silk tie, Charlotte's heart clenched. The sight of him never failed to take her breath away. His designer suit stretched across his broad shoulders and that hint of a smile he always seemed to possess gave the impression that he was plotting something and only he knew the secret. He had that same smile in bed.

Perhaps that subtle charm was the appeal that first drew her to him. That aura of mystery, those dark gray eyes that penetrated deep into her soul and left her tingling down to her toes.

As he looked into the camera and began to speak from the teleprompter, it seemed as if he was looking right at her.

She wanted something miraculous to come from these ninety days. Wanted the marriage repaired, legal guardianship of Lily and the perfect family life she'd always dreamed about. Even though she told Anthony they weren't getting back together, she couldn't lie to herself. She wanted him back, desperately. But not if he couldn't change. She dreamed of the day he became the husband and father she needed him to be.

Unfortunately, dreams and reality were so far apart, they were in separate hemispheres.

And this reality—the one with the man she loved so close, yet so far—was crushing her soul and shattering her heart. But unless Anthony made a huge turnaround, she would be gone at the end of the three months.

"He really is a good man," Charlotte told Lily, trying to force back the tears. "His priorities are just in the wrong order for this marriage to work."

She glanced from the television to Lily, who had one pudgy hand wrapped around the bottle and another clutching her silky pink blanket. Her lids fluttered down as her little lips pulled against the nipple of the bottle.

"Don't worry, little one," Charlotte whispered. "He knows how important you are. He won't let you down."

Of that Charlotte would see to herself. Neglecting a wife was one thing, but an innocent child…simply intolerable. Though she seriously doubted Anthony would do that to Lily. He had dropped everything when Rachel had passed and gone to retrieve the baby before she could spend another minute in the hands of social workers.

He'd also nearly begged her to give him ninety days so they could make Lily a comfortable, stable home. That said a lot for a man who allowed his work to rule every part of his life. She knew there was good in him. Knew how much family meant to him. So why had he taken her for granted the past few years?

Did he have any idea how that made her feel? That constant brushing aside, as if he just assumed she'd always be around at the end of the day. Obviously, in his mind, she was no better than a faithful golden retriever.

He'd taken her loyalty for granted and she'd allowed it. By not speaking up for herself, she had to take part of the blame for this broken marriage.

Charlotte swore she'd only watch a minute of the awards, but that minute turned into an hour. The bottle had long since been drained and Lily rested peacefully snuggled against Charlotte's chest.

As the awards drew to a close, Anthony stood in front of the camera once again and began to speak. Charlotte turned the TV up just a notch, so as not to wake Lily.

"Another great year of winners and nominees," he said with that heart-stopping smile. "With all the thanks going out, I have to take a moment and thank my beautiful wife, Charlotte, for staying home to be with our niece. Love you both."

He went on to announce the final presenters, but Charlotte didn't hear the rest. She stared at the screen, mouth open and a bit teary-eyed at how he'd publicly acknowledged her and Lily. He'd obviously been thinking of her, hoping she'd be watching.

This was the way things should have been. A house filled with babies running around—the proof of their love—and him combining his personal and professional lives.

Was fate dangling this second chance in front of her only

to mock her dreams? She'd have loved it if he'd come to her door and asked her to give him another chance. A blossom of hope had bloomed when she'd seen him, but he hadn't been there just for her. She'd have given anything had he dropped everything for their marriage.

Well, he had sent flowers, a rather impressive bouquet of her favorite lilies and roses, but he'd been away on business when they'd arrived. Had he brought them himself, made a little more of an attempt to gain her attention, he might have actually gotten that attention. Throwing money around was too easy…especially because he had so much of it to throw.

But he'd only needed her for the baby. His desperation had been fueled by fear, not love.

She'd been disappointed when he'd been packing yesterday, but at the same time she wasn't surprised. He was always needed somewhere that wasn't their home and always willing to jump to meet everyone else's demands.

Yesterday she'd walked into their master bedroom—*his* master bedroom—to have a serious talk, but once she'd seen the suitcase, her heart had fallen and the words on her lips had died. Evidently his trip hadn't warranted a heads-up and he just expected her to go along with his plans, as usual. His work was more important than anything outside the film industry.

But he'd mentioned her on TV as if they were a happily married couple. She knew Anthony well enough to know he would pull out all the stops to fight for what he wanted. But would his actions be sincere or simply because he didn't like rejection or loss? Perhaps he only mentioned them to throw off all the tabloids discussing their separation.

So much swirled through her mind. With all the problems of their marriage, having a crisis in private was nearly impossible. There was just so much worry and fear filling her.

And just because her period was five days late, didn't mean she needed to jump to conclusions. She'd been stressed lately and had a lot going on in her life. There was no reason to panic. Didn't she have enough on her plate without borrowing trouble?

In the morning, if there was still no sign, she'd go get a home test. Then when Anthony returned, she'd know whether or not they'd need to talk about more than Lily and their separation.

Wouldn't that just be the icing on the cake? Another baby.

Make that icing, sprinkles and a cherry on top.

Charlotte jostled a fussy Lily, replaying the life-changing events of her morning.

What a way to start off her day.

She'd woken after a fitful night of sleep and asked Monique to keep an eye on the baby while she ran a quick errand. No way was she going to ask anyone else to get the over-the-counter test. This was Hollywood. The last thing she needed was reporters getting wind of this.

This being the pregnancy test she'd taken in the drugstore restroom, because she couldn't wait until she was home. It was positive.

Who knew your life could change in the bathroom of a drugstore? It had taken some deep breathing and a shaky hand supporting her against the sink for several minutes before she could pull her gaze away from the two pink lines that had stared back at her.

She knew taking a pregnancy test in a drugstore bathroom was not the classiest of moves, but she hadn't wanted to risk anyone on her staff seeing it, or worse, the paparazzi. Juicy stories made for big bucks, so Dumpster diving wasn't above the paparazzi.

There was no privacy when you were married to Hollywood's hottest director, which was how she'd found herself huddled away in a one-room drugstore bathroom. Bad enough she'd had to wear a hat and oversized sunglasses, and use cash so she didn't have to flash her name on her credit card, but then she'd looked at the stick.

Once she could speak and not risk hyperventilating, Charlotte called her doctor, who assured her they did walk-in blood tests and to come on in.

Three hours later she was back home, waiting for the doctor's office to call with those results, but she knew what they would say. The same thing both drugstore pregnancy tests had said—because she'd bought the box of two just to be sure.

And now she swayed back and forth with a fussy Lily, wondering how she would tell Anthony when he returned from his trip. Which should be anytime now if he kept his word and came straight home.

Good Lord. She sounded like his mother, not his wife. Make that soon-to-be ex. What did it matter what he did with his time now? It was all the time before she'd left him that had mattered. All those years before she'd visited her attorney that Anthony couldn't give back to her.

Tears pricked her eyes and there was nothing she could do to prevent them from falling. Might as well join in with Lily.

"Shh," she whispered. "It'll be okay. Everything will work itself out."

Charlotte didn't know if she was consoling the baby or herself, but everything would be okay…she hoped.

Now she had a marriage not just on the rocks, but on the verge of falling off the cliff. In addition, she would become Lily's legal guardian in ninety days, she still had the Children's Hospital wing dedication and charity dinner to finish planning, and if all of that weren't enough to make her run straight out of the Hollywood Hills, now she was having a baby of her own with a man she loved but couldn't stay with.

Would Anthony even want another child? How would he handle two when for years he hadn't wanted any at all?

"Charlotte?"

Anthony's questioning tone came from downstairs and pulled her from all the thoughts bouncing around in her head.

"I'll be down in a minute," she called back.

Charlotte stared at herself in the mirror. She may be the same woman she had been this morning, but she certainly didn't feel the same. Her life had just taken another major come-out-of-nowhere blow and now she had to figure out how to deal with not one, but two babies and a possible divorce.

Or an even worse possibility—what if she miscarried again? How could she cope with another stab to the heart and loss like the last time? How much could one person truly handle before breaking?

Could her life be more of a mess?

She couldn't tell Anthony about the baby yet. Fear of losing the baby and fear of their future held her back.

She'd obviously conceived when Anthony had come to "talk" last month, so that would make her four weeks along. Her miscarriage had occurred at seven weeks.

To keep Lily's life as stable as possible and to see how seriously Anthony took his paternal responsibilities, she wouldn't say anything yet. There were so many reasons to keep this baby a secret, but most of all to keep her own sanity. She just couldn't pile another emotional issue on and give Anthony more leverage to make her stay. She wanted, needed him to stay for the right reasons.

Lily gave up fussing and moved straight into a full-throated cry with actual tears. Charlotte had the overwhelming urge to sit on the bed and join in, but that would solve nothing. And because Charlotte had never been one to sit around and cry when action needed to be taken, she straightened her shoulders and gave Lily an extra hug.

"Let's go get you a bottle, sweetheart."

Shifting the baby onto her hip, Charlotte padded out of her room and ran right into Anthony, who was standing outside her door.

"Oh." She stepped back. "I didn't know you were out here waiting for us."

He hadn't slept, or if he had, it was only for a few hours on his flight from New York to L.A. His eyes were red-rimmed, his hair a bit mussed and he still had on the dress pants and shirt he'd worn for the awards. He'd lost the tie and jacket and unbuttoned the top two buttons, the sleeves folded taut over his muscular forearms. Why he didn't change on his plane was beyond her.

Charlotte couldn't help but feel a twinge of sympathy for the man who was going to try to do it all in an attempt to prove to her that he could do it all.

Lily let out a loud wail.

"I need to feed her," Charlotte explained, moving past Anthony.

"I'll do it." He slid the baby from her grasp and started toward the stairs. "I haven't been spit up on for a couple days. I almost missed the smell."

No matter what life threw at him, Anthony always kept his sense of humor. As she followed him down the wide staircase, she recalled that his humor had been one of the traits that had led her to fall in love with him in the first place.

A lump of guilt rose in her throat over keeping news of their baby from him, but the man had never even entertained the idea of kids before. Work had always been his fallback excuse.

So now wasn't the time to reveal the truth. She needed to come to grips with this and figure out just how she was going to deal with this unexpected development. And he needed to get used to Lily before she hit him with the news of another baby.

Unexpected or not, Charlotte already loved this baby she carried. Children had always been her passion. In her volunteer work at the Children's Hospital, she fell in love on a daily basis with some remarkable kids.

Walking toward the kitchen, Charlotte trailed behind Anthony as he tried to shift a very red-faced Lily. The jostling really wasn't working—she was screaming louder—but he'd figure it out. All Charlotte could see was Lily's little head bobbing up and down to the rhythm of Anthony's awkward bounce.

He needed to do this, to work on being a dad, so he could see exactly what he was getting into.

He filled a bottle with filtered water and went to get the lid off the formula. "It's okay, Lily. I'm getting it."

Charlotte resisted the urge to take the baby, mix the bottle and put an end to everyone's misery. He was going to need all the practice he could get for when their own baby arrived— God willing. Still, her take-charge nature made it hard to do nothing. And since he was so set on proving to her that he could and would indeed be Superdad, she crossed her arms and leaned against the tiled center island.

Just as he balanced Lily in one arm and jerked the lid off the formula, the powder shot across the counter and down onto the gleaming hardwood floor. Unable to handle poor Lily's hunger cries another minute, Charlotte stepped up. Silence and self-control be damned.

"Let me do it." She scooped out the remaining formula from the canister and mixed the bottle. "Let me have her."

"I was getting it," he told her, relinquishing hold of his niece. "No need to take over."

Lily's pudgy hands reached for the bottle and the instant she started sucking, her cries ceased. Silence enveloped them and Charlotte found herself staring back into Anthony's rich gray eyes.

"There was no need to have her so upset when we both know I can make the bottle faster."

Charlotte started to move from the kitchen when he grabbed her shoulder to turn her back around.

"Is this how it's going to be?" he demanded. "For the next few months are you going to undercut every attempt I make at trying to help, to show you that I can do this? Are you so determined to leave me that you won't even give me the chance to prove myself as a husband or a father?"

Charlotte kept her gaze on the blissfully happy baby. No way could she look into his eyes right now. Not when he sounded so broken, yet so determined. She didn't want his words to get to her. She couldn't afford to lay her heart on the line again as far as Anthony was concerned. There were only so many times she could push her hurt aside and forgive him.

"I'm not undercutting anything," she told him. "I just wanted her fed."

He stepped closer, so close the arm she'd wrapped around Lily brushed against the hard plains of his abdomen. Beneath that cotton dress shirt lay rippled muscles that she'd explored with both her hands and her mouth. There wasn't a part of his body she hadn't seen or touched, but just that slight bit of contact sent a shiver rippling through her. He could always turn her on.

"I want to help. I need to." He laid a hand over hers on Lily's little belly. "Let me."

Charlotte's chest constricted at the warmth of his touch, his tone. He was holding out the olive branch…all she had to do was take it. All she had to do was look up into those smoky eyes and work with him, meet him in the middle. But pride, stubbornness and all those years of extending her own branch only to have it knocked aside had her shaking her head.

"I've got it."

And with that she walked out.

Some might say she was being difficult, some might accuse her of being hardheaded, and she would absolutely, 100 percent agree. She was all of that and much more. But time after time of being torn down, ignored and neglected would do that to a woman.

Not only could Anthony make her burn hotter than anyone, he also brought out the spiteful, surly side of her. And while she may be physically attracted to him still, she had serious questions about her love. The idea that she fell out of love made her sick to her stomach, but she just couldn't love a man who didn't love her enough to make her the top priority in his life.

If Charlotte thought that his sincerity would last for more

than a week, a month, she'd jump at the chance to meet him in the middle. But she knew how he was. She knew that nothing and no one would come between him and his precious work schedule—all the parties and awards ceremonies and the next big blockbuster film. And even if he decided he wanted to put her first, agents, managers, A-list actors and countless other people would eat up so much of his time, how would the man have any left for her or these children?

Yes, she'd definitely made the right decision in not telling him about the baby. He needed to seriously reshuffle his priority list before she would smack him with more life-altering news.

Even though this circumstance was different, she still needed to wait to tell him about the baby. The first time she'd gotten pregnant she hadn't told him because he'd been away filming. She'd planned a surprise for his return with a dinner and a little present. She'd bought a tacky T-shirt that said #1 Dad.

But she'd miscarried before she could make her announcement and before he returned from location. She'd tossed the T-shirt—gift bag and all—into the fire pit on their patio and cried as the ashes blew around and floated away, much like her dreams. Symbolic, really, that her dreams had literally gone up in smoke.

She'd faced that monumental, heartbreaking time alone. But this time he was here and he deserved to know, just not yet. They had a lot on their plate and they needed to deal with all the upcoming decisions together as a family, broken or not. And she would include him in the decision making as soon as she felt comfortable with the man he claimed he could be.

As Charlotte moved back through the marble foyer and up the stairs to lay Lily down for her afternoon nap, she heard Anthony's footsteps behind her.

"We need to talk," he told her as they reached the landing.

She couldn't agree more, so she nodded. "Let me get Lily settled and I'll come find you."

His eyes roamed over her face, landing on her lips. "I'll wait in our room."

He strode past her before she could correct him. It wasn't *their* room anymore. That beautiful master suite with a walk-out balcony, shower big enough for ten people and a sunken Jacuzzi would never be hers again. The day she'd walked out, she'd left behind any and all luxuries she'd grown accustomed to.

Of course, she would've given all of it up in a heartbeat if she could have had the man she'd married back in her life. To have that attentive, loving, funny guy back, she'd gladly turn her back on this "glamorous" lifestyle.

Not so glamorous once the cameras stopped filming and the doors to the mansion closed. Everyday problems still occurred for the rich and famous. She'd always heard the expression "More money, more problems." How true. Except their problems were out there for the public to see. Nothing was sacred in Hollywood, which made heartache that much harder to deal with.

Why had she once thought that they'd live happily ever after? Had she been that naive to think love would carry them over any obstacle?

Charlotte sat in the cushioned wooden rocker and eased back and forth while Lily finished her bottle. Sweet little lips pulled at the last drop of formula, then her mouth lost suction as she drifted off to sleep. Charlotte smiled, pulled the empty bottle away and eased the baby up onto her shoulder.

Keeping with the rocking motion, Charlotte closed her eyes and relished the peaceful bliss of holding a sleeping, innocent baby. No matter what happened with the marriage or the baby she carried, Charlotte knew she had a responsibility to Lily. Even though they weren't blood-related, that didn't matter. Charlotte would love and care for Lily as if she were her own.

Rachel had been an amazing woman. Charlotte hadn't been super-close with her sister-in-law because of the miles between them, but they had communicated a great deal over the phone.

Rachel had been so excited when she'd become pregnant. Charlotte had been both thrilled and a little jealous, and once she'd seen how happy the news made Anthony, she couldn't help but wonder if he'd changed his mind about having kids of his own.

But when she'd brought it up, he'd blown her off again, claiming it wasn't good timing. Good timing or not, he soon would have to get used to the idea of baby number two.

Giving in to the inevitable and relinquishing the peacefulness of rocking Lily, Charlotte came to her feet, laid Lily in her sleigh crib and went down the hall to her old master bedroom.

She prayed for the strength and courage to have a calm, adult conversation with Anthony. Prayed they wouldn't start yelling and hurling accusations.

She was getting stronger in standing up for herself and he needed to understand that unless and until he made a drastic change in his work ethic, she couldn't consider them a family.

Four

Charlotte entered her room—no, Anthony's room—but didn't see him. She moved farther in, beyond the sitting area and out on the balcony, where he'd left the French doors open. Everything about this room screamed *sexy*—from the delicate white sheers flowing from the patio doors and windows to the draped fabric encasing the canopy bed, the soft hues covering the wall, and the sunsets that would cast a romantic glow every evening.

Reality check. She wasn't here for romance. There was nothing romantic about being in a predicament where you were forced to work with someone you needed distance from, or loving someone with your whole heart only to have that love taken for granted and ignored.

Anthony stood against the short, fat pillars and marble rail, his back to her, his eyes on the lush grounds below that were manicured to perfection. There wasn't one aspect of this home that she hadn't had a hand in deciding when they'd built. She wondered if he even noticed that, before she left, she'd had a whole new flower garden and waterfall put in. If he had, he never mentioned it. Neglect had come on so many levels.

"I won't live these next three months like this," he said without turning. "I won't worry about making you angry or doing something wrong with Lily."

Charlotte wanted to go to the rail, but she remained in the doorway. If he was ready to open up and discuss his feelings without her begging him, she certainly wasn't going to interrupt.

"I love Lily," he went on, turning to face her. "I'm going to screw things up—I'm only human. But I'm trying my hardest here, so let me."

Unable to remain at a distance, Charlotte stepped forward and rested her hands next to his on the rail. "I know you love her—it would be impossible not to. But you can't just expect me to believe that this baby has turned your entire mind-set around. Our problems can't be fixed overnight because we instantly have a family. If anything, we have more than we expected."

She resisted the urge to run a hand over her flat stomach.

"I didn't say anything was fixed overnight." He pushed off the rail, his face mere inches from hers. "But you're here. I'm here. And I want to work through this, Charlie. Tell me you'll work with me and not against me."

Tears pricked her eyes, burned her throat. "I have no choice but to work with you now. But I can't promise that after this ninety-day period I'll still be living here."

He prayed for a miracle to take place in these next few months. "Let's take this one day at a time, okay? That's all I'm asking." All he was begging. "I just want us to be happy."

"It's hard to be happy right now, Anthony. We were separated, heading for divorce, then thrown into parenthood with Lily, and are reluctantly living together again. Kind of hard to celebrate anything."

Which reminded him of the surprise he had for her. He

needed to make her see that she and Lily *did* come first. Why couldn't he have both career and family? He'd damn well make this work. This was the only chance in life he had to get this right. He'd prove to himself—and Charlotte—that he could, in fact, have it all and excel at being a parent and a husband. Maybe he hadn't wanted children before, but fate had handed him a gift. Yes, he was worried, but he also knew he could do this…with Charlotte by his side.

"We're getting away," he blurted out. "Before I left for the awards, I had my assistant clear my schedule for the next two weeks. We're going to our house in Tahoe."

Charlotte's face brightened, then she tilted her head and raised one perfectly arched brow. "Really? Why now?"

He shrugged, hating that something so simple could have her so happy and skeptical at the same time. "I know we need time away from this lifestyle if I ever want a chance at a family and happiness with you. I know how much you love Tahoe, so we're going. Originally, I was only going to go for a few days, but I think we'll stay longer."

Charlotte closed her eyes, the breeze blowing her long blond hair back over her shoulder. The sun kissed her face, and Anthony knew how lucky he was. He'd taken her for granted, but he was also very aware of everything she loved about life. Now he just had to present all that love to her. She deserved everything he could give…and he had finally realized that didn't mean material things, which he'd always lavished on her in the past, instead of sharing his time and feelings with her.

"Can you be ready to leave by tomorrow morning?" he asked.

Her face turned back to his, unshed tears on the verge of spilling over. "I can. Thank you for doing this."

As she turned to go, Anthony grabbed for her arm. "Stay. Don't always be the first to walk from a room because you're afraid I will."

A sad smile formed on her full lips. "Won't you? You've

always walked away, Anthony. It's hard seeing your back so much as the distance grows between us."

Guilt crept up and squeezed his chest, but he deserved the hurt. He needed to use it to make himself and their marriage stronger.

"I could say I'm sorry, and I'd mean it," he told her. "But I know words will do very little at this point. I plan on showing you that I'm worthy of being a good father to Lily, and the husband you need."

Her eyes darted down to his hand on her bare arm. "This is harder than I thought," she whispered. "Being here, with you. I want so much, but I can't hope, can't dream for things that may never be."

"You used to confide all your dreams in me." He closed the space between them, keeping his hand on her arm. "Don't shut me out, Charlie. I'm trying. I've never stopped loving you. The film sets, movie premieres, awards shows—none of that can fill my heart the way you do."

"Then why haven't you shown me?" she asked, her voice cracking from emotion. "Why do you always put work first?"

He brought his other hand up to cup her cheek. He'd missed that silky skin, that hitch in her breath when he barely caressed his fingertips over her jawline. He missed making love to her and holding her in his arms while she slept. And the one frenzied night they'd shared a month ago didn't help. Once she'd asked him to leave, he realized just how much he wanted her back…how much he missed holding her in his arms.

He'd taken her and their marriage for granted. There was no sugarcoating it. Until she left, he hadn't realized how much she filled his life.

"I never thought I was," he confessed. "I was just doing my job and knew you'd be home when I came back. I can't apologize for my work, because it's who I am. All I can do is show you I can put you and Lily first. But, at the same time, I can't turn my back on who I am."

"I don't want you to forget who you are," she told him, looking into his eyes. "I never meant for you to give up what you love, Anthony. I guess I should've been more vocal about that. But your priorities…"

"Right now I have only one priority."

He captured her lips, keeping his touch light because he knew that made her weak. She'd always loved the tender moments. So many times they'd made love in a frantic hurry, but he knew her better than she knew herself. And wasn't that the message he'd been missing? She loved when he took his time with her, showed her real love.

With a stroke of his fingertips up her arm and over the gooseflesh he'd caused, he laid his palm on the small of her back and eased her against his body.

Yeah, he knew her so well. Just one feather-soft kiss had her sighing, leaning into him.

He missed the feel of her flush against him while he slept. Missed the way he would wake her in the night when he needed to feel that connection he could only get from her.

Unable to keep the kiss light, Anthony tilted his head and took more. Charlotte's fingers dug into his shoulders, her breasts flattened against his chest.

How could she walk away from him, from this? They had so much heat between them. And now they had Lily to keep them together for a minimum of ninety days. He intended to take advantage of every moment.

Fatherhood may have been something he'd always feared he'd fail at. Maybe because he'd been so successful with his career, he was afraid of not being able to do the same in his personal life. He had no idea why it scared him so much. No doubt the shrink Charlotte wanted him to see would be able to pin down a reason after the first session. But now that Lily was in their lives, he knew he'd do anything to keep his family together. Fear or no fear, he had an obligation and he wasn't backing down.

So if he had to give in and go to therapy, then so be it. He couldn't, *wouldn't* live without his family.

Charlotte pushed away, dropping her hands. "You don't play fair."

He stared at her swollen lips, more than ready to taste them again. "I don't plan to. I want you back, Charlie. In every sense of the word."

Stepping back farther, she licked her lips. "I'm going to start packing."

Selfishly he took comfort in knowing she was running scared. That kiss hadn't left her unaffected. But he'd let her think she was in control...for now.

"You may want to avoid this," he said, motioning between them. "But you can't avoid me when we're in Tahoe. It'll just be me, you and Lily. I've given the staff paid vacations."

Charlotte winced as if that were a bad thing. "Not a good idea."

He couldn't help but smile. "And why is that?" Leaning back against the marble rail, he crossed his arms over his chest. "Afraid we won't be able to keep our hands off each other?"

That defiant chin tilted. "That's not it at all.... I just..."

His smile grew as she stammered for an excuse to cover the lie. He knew she feared being alone with him. Knew he'd break her down, win her back. She worried that her heart would get broken once more. But he refused to let that happen. He'd never willingly hurt her again.

"I'm not going to explain myself," she finally said. "I'll be in my room."

As she spun on her heel, he called out, "Don't forget to pack that red nightie I bought you last Christmas."

She marched through the French doors, across the master suite, and slammed the door. A second later Lily sent up a wail.

Ah, yes. This was going to be an interesting vacation.

Packed and ready to go, Charlotte couldn't help but feel a spurt of hope for this trip. She knew it was a lot to lay so much pressure on one getaway, but Anthony had never suggested they go away so they could work on things. If he was willing to try, then how could she not?

At the same time, she also had to be realistic. Years of poor communication, when there even *was* any communication, could not be repaired in a few weeks. But it was a start and that counted for something.

The doctor's appointment came first, though. This was one of those times she was thankful her name and status moved things along. They were able to squeeze her in for a prenatal appointment. She had told Anthony she had an appointment at the hospital and he'd just assumed she meant the Children's Hospital. She hadn't corrected him. She'd simply said she shouldn't be too long and when she came back they could leave.

God, she loathed lying, but, at this stage, how could she open up? Fear of a miscarriage and fear of Anthony not changing drove her to keep the truth to herself…at least for now.

In retrospect, he'd deserved to know about the last baby, but she'd never uttered a word. Selfishly she'd kept that to herself because she'd been so hurt and angry that he hadn't been there when she needed him most. But her doctor's appointment had gone well, and now she was heading home to get ready to go away with her family.

But right now she was going to concentrate on Lily and this time with Anthony in Tahoe.

She so loved their Tahoe getaway home—this one more so than the others. The Tahoe home was away from all the hustle and bustle of a big city and provided a nice relaxing escape. Just what they needed.

Countless times she would go away on her own to enjoy the serenity, the beauty. Several occasions when planning a charity event, this tranquil home had provided a nice place to think. Unlike when she worked in Hollywood and their version of beauty was skewed and molded by plastic surgeons and trophy wives.

Charlotte opened the door to her Hollywood Hills home and saw her two pieces of matching luggage sitting by the door. Anthony must've brought them down from her room. She reached to pick them up when his voice stopped her.

"If you're ready I can take your bags." Charlotte turned to see Anthony descending the grand staircase. "I just wanted to make sure you didn't have any last-minute items you wanted to pack."

"No, I'm good to go." She smiled. "I packed light, since I still have some stuff up there from my last visit."

He tilted his head. "When was that?"

"Right after I moved out. I knew you were going out of town and I wanted to be alone and surrounded by nothing but nature, instead of glitz and glamour. I was only there for a few days because I had to get back to the hospital."

The way he studied her face, the muscle ticking in his jaw, had her wondering what he was thinking. But with the way she'd stipulated things between them during this ninety-day period, she didn't feel as if it was her place to ask.

Wasn't she the one who wanted this separation to move forward? She couldn't probe his private thoughts and still expect some distance.

Once upon a time, in the beginning, she wouldn't have had to ask. But communication had slowly become an issue. Little by little their lives became routine, resulting in bottled-up feelings and hurts that led them here…on the verge of divorce with two babies…one of which was still a secret.

But isn't that how all marriages ended? Slowly? They never came to an abrupt halt. Bad decisions, no matter how small, piled on top of each other, would break down even the strongest of marriages.

"Lily is playing in her crib if you want to grab her. I'll meet you in the car," he told her, reaching for her suitcase. "Her things are already loaded. When I asked my assistant to cancel my appointments, I also asked her to have the staff set up a room with a crib and anything else we'll need."

A little piece of her melted as she realized how much thought he'd put into this trip. "Thank you."

Before she could focus too much on how he was taking care of his family in all the right ways, Charlotte moved past him and headed to get Lily. The cooing from the nursery had her smiling despite the turmoil in her heart. This trip might be strained, and if things didn't go well it might be the final straw in this marriage, but one thing was certain—Lily would not suffer. Nor would this baby she carried.

But, she vowed to herself, she'd go into this trip and the next several weeks with an open mind. Anthony had asked for ninety days and she was going to see what happened. Because she still loved him, she'd see where this led. But she also had to see a vast turnaround or they would have no foundation to stand on with their new beginning.

Lily's crib sat on the farside of the room, beneath the colorful painting of the two little girls playing. When Charlotte had painted the image, she'd been hoping one day those would be her girls. She laid a hand over her flat stomach, hoping, wishing.

She looked down at Lily, who was lying on her back, chewing on a pink stuffed elephant without a care in the world. And that's how Charlotte intended to keep Lily's life. These babies would not worry about stability…no matter what the end result with Anthony was.

Charlotte's childhood had never been stable. With her junkie dad and a mother who worked sometimes three jobs to support them, her upbringing was less than a Norman Rockwell painting. Added to that, when her twin sister had gotten sick and passed, Charlotte had been left feeling alone and abandoned. She'd vowed to always make sure her children knew love and stability.

"Hey, sweetheart." Charlotte leaned in and picked up Lily,

bringing the soggy animal with her. "You ready for a trip? Uncle Anthony has a special getaway planned for us."

She checked the diaper, surprised to find it completely dry... and nearly falling off from the loose fit. Anthony had obviously tried to wrestle Lily into a dry diaper before the trip.

Charlotte suppressed a laugh at the image. He'd yet to master putting the diaper on without Lily screaming and his muttering how hard changing a diaper was.

She laid Lily down on the changing table and adjusted the tabs for a more secure fit.

"There we are, sweetheart," she said, picking up the baby. "He tried, so we have to give him credit."

The weight of the baby in her arms had her anxious for her own. She'd be lying if she didn't admit she was nervous about miscarrying again. But how could she not be excited? Yes, the timing was terrible, and who knew what life this baby would come into, but was there ever a perfect time to become a parent? Considering that life was full of ups, downs and uncertainties, probably not.

When Charlotte met Anthony at the car, he opened her door and motioned. "After you," he told her, taking Lily. "I'll strap her in."

Shocked, Charlotte stared as Anthony pulled Lily from her grasp and eased her into the car seat. He only struggled with the buckles for a minute before figuring it out, and Lily only whimpered for a bit while Anthony had her.

Maybe this trip would be good for all of them. Getting used to a baby was a big step, and time away from the media and the hubbub of their daily lives would be good for Lily.

"I think she's adjusting well," Charlotte said once Anthony got in and started the luxury SUV. "She seems happy."

"She's too young to know much else. I hate to say it, but she'll never remember Rachel. And that may be for the best. At least she won't have that heartache."

Like the heartache he was feeling. The unspoken words hung in the air.

Tears pricked her eyes at the thought of her sister-in-law never experiencing all the things Lily would face in life.

"It just breaks my heart," Charlotte whispered. "A child without her mother."

Anthony's hand reached toward her, hesitated and moved back onto the steering wheel. Turning her head to look out the window, Charlotte pretended that she hadn't noticed the gesture. She wished he'd followed through. His touch, so warm, so familiar, was something she missed. Charlotte knew that if she and Anthony were going to have a chance at happiness, they'd have to weave their way carefully through the minefield of emotions.

She also had to steel herself. Being under the same roof with Anthony would test her willpower like nothing else.

For three months she'd lived without him. For three months she'd cried herself to sleep over a marriage she'd tried so hard to hold on to, but her wishes hadn't been enough to keep it together.

"Hopefully, Lily will stay entertained with her teething book," he said, cutting into her thoughts. "We can stop for a picnic lunch once we get closer to Tahoe."

The image lifted her spirits. Charlotte turned back around, smiling. "Picnic? What did the cook make us?"

"Actually, I put together some sandwiches and stuff for us." He threw her a glance and winked. "I have many surprises in store during our trip, and I'm doing it on my own. No staff."

"I'm impressed," she told him.

Charlotte was almost afraid to ask what his other surprises entailed. If she knew Anthony, he'd try to "surprise" her back into his bedroom. And heaven knew she'd love to be there, but she just couldn't give in.

No matter how much her hormones were out of whack.

Five

Once the picnic was over, they headed toward their home in Tahoe. And that's how Anthony would always think of the six-thousand-square-foot getaway—*theirs*. They shared everything and would continue to do so because there was no way he would give in to a divorce after these ninety days. Divorce mean quitting, giving up, and he'd never been a fan of either one.

But if he played his cards right, Charlotte wouldn't even consider leaving. He'd been married to her for so long, he knew what she liked and what he could say to make her smile, laugh…or follow him to bed.

Granted he hadn't paid that much attention to her over the past few years because he'd been busy, but that passionate, desirable woman was still inside—he had no doubt.

He'd let monotony run his life, assuming Charlotte would always be there while he tended to other things. He'd gotten so caught up with work, then spending time with the Danes. He'd been so concerned with impressing other people that he'd forgotten to keep impressing his wife, to keep her from falling out of love with him.

Had she indeed fallen out of love?

He shook himself. She'd agreed to do this trip, hadn't she? He refused to believe she'd completely given up.

And he knew she wasn't totally unaffected by his touch. He hadn't missed the way the pulse at the base of her throat quickened when he moved in close. And when he'd kissed her, her breath had caught a split second before she leaned into him.

Guilt struck him, constricting his heart. He knew his wife better sexually than emotionally. Oh, at one time he knew all the various levels of Charlotte, but now, well, now he wasn't so sure.

He was confident, though, that when it came to life, Charlotte still loved the simple things. And even that simple kiss had heated him in places that only she could touch. She'd always had a simplicity about her. She had basic wants, needs, desires. He intended to fulfill each of those and more during their time away.

And there his mind went again to the sexual side of their relationship. Yes, they had amazing chemistry, but he wanted his wife to fall in love with him all over again. He wanted to win her heart, not just her body.

While in Tahoe, he had some surprises for her. He knew just what to do to get her to let her guard down and relax. That's one of the reasons he'd asked the staff to give them privacy. Charlotte needed for him to get back to the basics of their marriage when it was just the two of them and life was simple. By *simple,* he meant that she'd never craved the limelight, never wanted to go out and have all the plastic surgeries that nearly every woman in Hollywood had. She was perfect the way she was…at least in his eyes. He'd never been into silicone breasts, bee-stung lips or tattooed-on makeup.

Which was why he'd had this home built just a few years back. They'd actually only been to the home twice together since it had been built, now that he thought of it. Sad, considering he wanted this to be for them to enjoy, but she'd been making trips alone.

"So, I never asked about your appointment this morning." He wanted her to talk, to discuss her life now. "How are things coming with the new medical wing at the Children's Hospital?" he asked, unable to handle the silence any longer.

"Quicker than I'd anticipated." She continued to stare out the side window, but at least she was talking to him. "We're hoping to have the ribbon-cutting ceremony in a couple of months."

"I'm sure they appreciate all you do for them," he told her.

On a sigh, Charlotte turned in her seat. "Anthony, you don't have to pretend to be interested in my volunteer work. There's no need to have strained conversations during this trip."

He shrugged. "I wasn't straining for a conversation. I legitimately wanted to know about your work and the wing. What you do isn't just important to you. I do care."

From the corner of his eye he saw her study him. He waited for her to say something.

"You've never seemed interested before."

Risking a glance her way, he saw confusion on her face and cursed himself for being so self-absorbed. "A mistake I hope to rectify. I want to know what you do with your time when I'm gone. I'm proud of you, Charlie."

She turned to look back out the window, but not before he heard the hitch in her breath.

"Something wrong?" he asked after another moment's silence.

"I've waited to hear you say that." Her voice cracked. "For years, I've wanted you to take an interest in what I do, to understand how important it is to me."

She turned to face him. "I know you want to try, but I'm scared, Anthony. I can't take more hurt if this doesn't work out. Right now I can't promise anything beyond these ninety days."

He let the matter drop, but there was no way in hell he'd

ever give up. If it took letting her think she was in control, then so be it. But he knew in his heart that he had to take back the reins of this relationship or he'd lose her forever.

Had he had that epiphany years ago, perhaps he wouldn't be in this situation—an instant parent with a wife volleying between confusion and divorce.

No way would he settle for a divorce. He'd never thought she'd leave him. He'd never considered the fact. He knew they had their share of problems, but what married couple didn't?

Obviously, the problems were bigger than he'd thought and the tabloids had picked up on that turmoil and run with it. They'd accused him of sleeping with his previous assistant, which had never happened. Mia had been more like a sister to him than anything. She was one amazing assistant, and he'd hated when she'd quit to go work for Olivia Dane. It was pure coincidence that he'd discovered Olivia was his birth mother around the same time. And pure bad luck that Mia had stumbled onto that information. He'd asked her to keep it to herself, which she had, but it couldn't have been easy.

But it turned out Olivia had known about him and kept tabs on him through the years. It warmed his heart to know that she'd watched his career grow.

His one-time hatred of her son, now his brother, Bronson Dane, had to have been a heavy burden on her. Anthony wouldn't go so far as to say he and Bronson were friends now, but they were civil to each other and Anthony was hoping for a miracle as far as this family was concerned.

Bronson and Olivia were getting ready to begin working on Olivia's biographical film, depicting her life from her early films to her final one. She had grace and elegance like no one else, and her timeless beauty made her the most famous Hollywood icon ever.

And Anthony was champing at the bit to be the director.

"What are you thinking?" Charlotte asked, pulling him from his thoughts.

"About Olivia," he answered, telling only part of the path his thoughts had traveled. "Just wondering how she handled all the public animosity between me and Bronson over the years. It couldn't have been easy on her."

"It wasn't easy on you, either," she told him in a soft, sad voice. "I never brought it up because I didn't think you wanted to talk about it."

"I'll talk now." He'd love to keep talking to her. He couldn't recall the last time they'd just talked. Normally, when they were alone, they were naked or arguing. "That's why we're going away."

"I hope so," she whispered.

With him driving, naked wasn't an option. And as for arguing, he wasn't in the mood to disagree with her, because most of what she said since their split was true. He hadn't been a good husband, at least not when it came to offering emotional support. As for monetary support, he knew no other man could've provided her with better things.

But that thought circled him back around to the fact his Charlie wasn't like most Hollywood debutantes. She didn't care about shopping sprees and Botox. She cared about people, and that made her all the more special.

She'd put her pride and her broken heart aside to give him ninety days because of Lily—that just proved that point. And he intended to make every moment count.

The second they pulled into the drive, Lily woke from her slumber.

For the past few hours Charlotte had been battling pregnancy hormones and the mounting tension from Anthony's attempt to play get-to-know-your-wife-in-twenty-questions.

She didn't want to feel uncomfortable in the same car as her husband. They'd shared a home, a life for nearly a decade, and now sharing a car ride had her stomach in knots.

Though she'd like to blame that on the morning sickness she'd had earlier.

Charlotte sighed and gazed out the window to the two-story "cabin." There were so many rustic mansions in the Tahoe area. Everybody wanted a piece of the beautiful serenity and laid-back lifestyle.

Well, everyone but her husband, who rarely came to Tahoe. She knew he'd initially had this place built for her…just another way to buy her love and affection. And while she wasn't turning down the breathtaking home, she would give it up—together with the Hollywood Hills mansion—in a second if that meant Anthony would love her without throwing money around to prove it. When and if she saw an action that came straight from his heart, she'd know how much she meant to him. That would be the day she would reconsider their separation and pending divorce.

Charlotte stared up at the second-story balcony that stretched across the length of the house. Three sets of patio doors led onto the balcony from each of the bedrooms, and Charlotte knew this would be the first time each of those bedrooms were occupied at the same time.

The sound of Lily's rattle shaking pulled Charlotte from thinking too much about being secluded with Anthony for two full weeks. Yet again, the priority had to be Lily and the baby she carried.

"Here we are, Miss Lily," Anthony said.

Charlotte got out and went to retrieve the baby while Anthony pulled out all the bags. After slipping the new pink-and-gray-plaid designer diaper bag over her shoulder, Charlotte closed the door and took Lily up the stone steps to the house.

"Maybe we can go swimming," she told Lily. "Would you like that? Your mama used to love to swim. Once we came up here for a weekend together, just us girls. Maybe you and I can do that sometime."

Tears pricked her eyes, knowing that Rachel would never be

here on another girls' weekend again. They'd only been on one trip a year ago, and then Rachel had gotten pregnant. As much as they'd tried to plan more getaways, life kept interfering and one excuse turned into another. And now here Charlotte was with a lot of regrets and an innocent child. Why hadn't she carved out more time for people and things that truly mattered?

If there was one thing Charlotte learned from Rachel's death, it was that she needed to live for today and live the life she wanted. And she wanted a life with Anthony, if only he could meet her halfway.

Please let this trip bring about a miracle.

"Can you get the key?"

Charlotte turned to see Anthony struggling with a suitcase in each hand and one tucked under each arm.

"Where is it?" she asked.

"My right pocket."

She stood motionless as he cocked a hip out for her to reach it. "You're kidding."

That smirk he'd thrown to so many cameras during interviews mocked her. "As you can see, my hands are full."

Charlotte closed the space between them and slid her hand into his pocket. "They're not in there."

He let out a low, sultry laugh. "My mistake. Must be the other one."

She looked him in the eye. Humor lurked there, but that wasn't the underlying emotion. Desire glared back at her, and Charlotte quickly thrust her hand in the other pocket and yanked the keys out.

"Ow," he said. "Be gentle."

Without letting him know how much his little game had affected her out-of-control hormones—damn hormones—she unlocked the door and turned off the alarm.

"Here we are, sweetheart." Charlotte glanced around the cozy home.

All the oversized leather furniture in the sunken living room appeared inviting. The large patio doors that led out to the pool allowed the afternoon sun to beam through. The last time she'd been up here she'd been inspired to paint an early morning view of the lake, a piece that now hung near the doors.

But it was the vase of fresh hydrangeas sitting on the squat coffee table between the sofas that caught her attention. From the doorway, she could see a card beside them.

"I thought the staff was gone." She turned to look at Anthony as he set the luggage inside the door.

"They are. I had them do a few things before they took off."

A few things—the surprises he'd mentioned in the car? Charlotte wanted to ask what, but she knew she'd find out soon enough. She couldn't help but let hope spread through her. He'd planned ahead, for her—that had her smiling and anticipating the next promised surprise. Holding tight to Lily, Charlotte eased toward the flowers and the card.

"To new beginnings and our beautiful family."

She swallowed a lump as tears pricked her eyes. Her favorite flowers and a card from Anthony, and she'd only walked in the door. She was interested to see what else he had in store.

"The flowers are beautiful. Thank you."

Anthony stepped down into the living area to stand beside her. "I mean what it says on the card. I want this to be a new beginning, Charlie. I want more than ninety days."

Tired from the car ride, tired from the pregnancy and tired of being at odds with her husband for so long, Charlotte yawned and rubbed her temple. "We just need to move cautiously, for everyone's sake."

He nodded, studying her face. "Here, give me Lily. Why don't you go lie down?"

Lily was pulled from her arms before she could answer. "Um...okay."

Lily started to fuss, reaching for Charlotte. When Anthony stepped back, Lily let out a full-fledged scream, turning her little cherub face red.

"Go," he urged, patting the baby's back. "I promise we'll be fine. We need to get used to each other."

Charlotte hesitated, feeling guilty, but knowing he was right. He and Lily did have to get used to each other. At this point they had no other choice.

"Promise you'll come get me if she doesn't calm down."

He lifted Lily up in the air and spun around in a circle, easing her wailing some, but not much.

"I swear," he promised. "If she gets out of control, I'll come get you."

Charlotte nodded, kissed Lily on the cheek and headed toward one of the guest bedrooms. She'd give Anthony their master suite. Even though she loved that suite with its king-sized canopy bed and overly large, open shower, she wasn't going to sleep in the same bed as her husband.

But she had a feeling he would do everything he could to make sure she ended up there before their time in Tahoe was over.

Six

"So the flowers didn't go over as well as I'd hoped, Lily Bug."

Anthony sat on the wooden swing on the back porch and swayed with his niece who had finally calmed down once he fed her a jar of puréed peaches and some of those puff snacks that smelled like sawdust.

He'd only left the high chair in the kitchen a minor disaster and intended to clean it up later. Right now he was enjoying spending quality time with his niece.

"I thought for sure the flowers would warrant a kiss on the cheek."

Lily stared up at him as he handed her more puff snacks. "You have no idea what I'm saying. As long as I keep feeding you, you'll love me. I finally figured out how to make you like me."

He looked out beyond the pool, patio and lush garden to the lake. He'd have to step up his game plan if he wanted to gain ground during this getaway.

He'd been surprised at how fast, and easy, it had been to

call his new assistant and have her shuffle things around so he could provide Charlotte with the time away from Hollywood that she needed. That he needed, as well. He needed to stop letting agents and actors consume all his time. God knew he was powerful enough to be calling the shots.

At the start of his career, he'd had to be available at all times to show how serious he was. But now, he knew, without being vain, that he was a big enough name that he could be choosy and clear his schedule whenever he wanted.

"What do you think we should do next?" He handed Lily a couple more snacks, her slobbery fingers greedily scooping them from his palm. "I have to say, I'm going to need your help. She may find my tactics sneaky, but I'm desperate."

He leaned down right in Lily's face. "But don't tell her I said that."

With the sun beating down on them, Anthony decided to make use of the pool. He'd never really enjoyed all the amenities he'd paid for. Why hadn't he made more time for the basics in life? Why hadn't he whisked his wife away on a relaxing trip instead of making all his traveling about business?

"Want to go swimming, Lily Bug?"

This would be an experience. Once he changed into his suit in the pool house, he scooped her up, took her back inside and retrieved her suit from her little suitcase with a monogrammed L on the front.

"Let's wrestle you into this," he said. He pulled her clothes off and tugged the tight blue-and-white polka-dot suit up over her chunky little legs. Surprisingly, she only fussed for a minute. But when he held her up and inspected her he frowned.

"Diaper or no diaper?"

The image of floaties in his pool had him cringing. "Diaper," he said to himself. "Definitely the diaper."

He went back to the pool house and slathered sunscreen all over her and even up into her wisps of dark hair. That much he knew. Sunscreen was a must for children. And just to be on the safe side, he topped her off with the hat that matched her suit.

Holding on to her tightly, he stepped a foot into the refreshing water and eased in. Lily jerked her feet up once her toes connected with the cooler water. Her lip quivered as she sucked in a breath.

"It's okay. I've got you."

And he knew she was too young to realize he was referring to life.

He splashed just a tad of the water up onto her legs to get her used to the temperature. "See? Isn't this nice?"

Walking around the shallow end, he occasionally bounced up and down so Lily could enjoy the water. Her initial whimpers soon turned to squeals and giggles and Anthony realized he'd never heard her do either of those things while he was holding her. So, food and pool—two things he could certainly handle. Praise God, a miracle had happened. If only Charlie were that easy to win over.

He hadn't realized how fun, how life-changing—in a positive way—a baby could be. So far, this experience of being a father was not as scary as he'd first thought. Remorse swept over him as he thought of all the times he'd used work as an excuse to keep his life a children-free zone.

He kept up the playfulness, wanting to hear more of her beautiful sounds…sounds Rachel was missing. She was missing all the happy faces, the muttering of wannabe words.

Anthony missed his sister with an ache he hadn't thought possible. He hated that she wouldn't see her baby grow up. He'd never understand why a life had to be cut short. He just couldn't wrap his mind around the fact that he was here and she wasn't.

He continued bouncing up and down until he caught sight of a flash of skin from the corner of his eye.

"Can I join you guys?"

Charlotte started into the pool wearing a string bikini. Anthony didn't know whether to thank God or Satan.

To his knowledge she didn't own a one-piece, but he had a feeling if she'd known about this little trip, she would've bought one just to torture him.

Or maybe she purposely put on the skimpiest one she owned to torture him. Either way, he was a sucker when it came to her body. All lush and curvy and so perfect when molded against his.

"Come on in. Lily Bug and I were just having fun." He splashed a little more water over Lily, making her laugh. "Did you have a good rest?"

"I did, but then I felt guilty for lying down, so I got up. I actually made a phone call to the caterer and the director of the hospital. I'm trying not to work while we're here, but there are a few details I left hanging for the dedication of the new wing."

He couldn't think of a response, not when the water settled just under her breasts, causing her nipples to pucker. He knew what lay beneath that slim scrap of fabric. He'd touched her, tasted her. And he would again soon. There was only so long his Charlie could hold out.

But he knew he had to take this slow. He wanted his wife back, and not just in his bed. He wanted to see her smile again and he wanted to be the one who put that smile on her face. He wanted that broken bond to be repaired and he wanted to move forward with their new family. He wanted it all, but before he could seduce her body, he had to seduce her heart. He wanted her to fall in love with him all over again.

"Did I hear you calling her Lily Bug?" she asked, moving closer to them.

He looked down at Lily who was patting the top of the water and blinking with each drop that threatened to get near her eyes. "Yes. It just came out at first, and now that's what I call her."

"I like it." Charlotte smiled and adjusted Lily's hat over her eyes. "Did you put plenty of sunscreen on her?"

"Of course."

"What about the swimming diapers?"

Swimming diapers? There were special diapers for swimming?

"She has on her regular diaper," he answered, knowing he'd done something wrong. "What's the difference?"

Charlotte took Lily from him and held her up out of the water to show a very wet, very saggy diaper. "This. If she'd had on a swimming diaper, it wouldn't absorb all the water and wouldn't be sagging practically to her ankles."

"Really?" He was a little amazed that a diaper could hold so much moisture and still stay on.

Oh, Lord. He knew he was already deep into fatherhood when a diaper impressed him.

It used to be that new special effects and lighting techniques in films would impress him. Now it was the absorbency of a diaper.

Yeah, that was quite a switch.

"Where are these magical diapers?" he asked.

Charlotte moved up the steps and out of the pool. Her response was totally lost on him because now those scraps of material she had on were wet and clinging to places his hands ached to touch. Water droplets slid down the back of her thighs over smooth, tanned skin.

"I'll be right back."

Charlotte took Lily inside where he assumed she'd packed these superabsorbent diapers. That should give him enough time to get in a couple laps, get his libido back under control and quit lusting after his own wife who was so close, yet still unapproachable when it came to intimacy.

Her hands shook as she pulled the swim diaper up over Lily's pudgy legs. When she'd glanced out her window and seen Anthony's bare, tanned, chiseled chest with Lily's pale body lying against it, she nearly drooled right there in the privacy of her room.

True, his sexy chest was nothing new. Impressive as it was, she never tired of looking at it. But it was the image of her big, strong husband with those powerful hands holding on to an innocent, sweet baby that had her heart clenching.

So, yeah, a little groan of desire had escaped her when she'd seen them together. And she figured if she had to be tortured by looking at him, she could play that game, too.

She'd pulled out his favorite bikini, the simple black one made up of only triangles and strings. Only after she'd gotten into the pool, she wasn't so sure that had been a good idea. They were both nearly naked and desire shot straight from his eyes as he raked his gaze over her heated body…her heated, aching body. She wondered if he noticed her heavier, fuller breasts. She remembered from the last pregnancy that her bras and shirts were a tad snug from the get-go. That was one of the first signs, other than her missed period, of the pregnancy.

But her bikini had never completely covered her top anyway, so maybe he hadn't noticed. He was a man, and this was his favorite suit on her, so she had no doubt he was cooling off out there in the pool.

The diaper was a good save, though if he'd had a swimmy diaper on Lily, Charlotte would've had to come up with another reason to beat a hasty retreat.

What was she thinking, toying around with lust like that? Her emotions were all over the place and she wished she could just pick one and go with it.

She pulled the bathing suit back over the baby and headed out to the pool.

"Let's just play on the steps, okay, little one?"

No way could she be that close to Anthony again and not touch him. And she knew if he'd risen from the pool, not only would she have seen how low his trunks fit around his narrow waist, she'd have seen one impressive erection.

She had to get these hormones under control. He was her husband, for pity's sake. She'd touched, tasted and savored his body countless times. Unfortunately, she'd read online that many women are more into sex when pregnant than any other time.

Perfect timing, Fate. Thanks a lot. Of all the times in her marriage to be extra horny...

"She's all ready," Charlotte announced in a perky voice, hoping to make this a more family-friendly, G-rated swim session. "We're going to splash around on the steps for a while."

Anthony smiled as he leaned an arm on the edging of the pool...thankfully at the other end. "She seems to like the water."

Charlotte sat on the second step and placed Lily on her lap. She squealed in delight and slapped her hands on top of the water, making Charlotte laugh.

"We need to get her some toys for the pool or one of those little inflatable rafts she can just sit in."

"I'll get it today," he replied.

Charlotte looked up at Anthony, who was moving through the water like a predator. So much for keeping their distance.

"You always enjoyed the water, too." He moved closer, standing at the base of the steps. Close enough that if she extended her legs just barely, her feet would brush his long legs. "If I recall, we enjoyed this pool together the last time we were in it. After that, we enjoyed the hot tub."

Charlotte turned her gaze from his. It would be so easy to keep looking in those eyes, to run back down that lane of memories, but she couldn't. No matter how much her body craved to make new pool memories.

"Don't do this, Anthony." She didn't raise her voice, she didn't beg. "We have to move slowly and you know it. We have more than just ourselves to think about."

He propped an arm on the concrete beside her and leaned closer to her face. "What I know is we are still married and we are sharing guardianship of Lily." He leaned next to her ear and whispered, "And I'm also positive that right now, you're trying very hard not to give in to this sexual pull between us."

Why did he have to know her so well? Why did he have to say all the right, or, in her opinion, wrong, words to make her hormones jump up and start screaming? God, how would he react if he knew about the baby she carried?

"It doesn't matter what my body wants, Anthony." She looked back up at him, keeping her eyes on his and not on that gorgeous chest inches away. "My heart is in control right now. It can't afford another beating and I won't let my emotions override what's best for Lily—and hopefully us—in the long run."

He slid her hair from her shoulder to settle behind her back. The gentle touch sent shivers through her body.

"I'm not putting my emotions above Lily's needs, either," he told her. "There's no reason we can't have it both ways."

She swallowed the lump of remorse. "There are about nine years of reasons we can't get into this. Nine years of problems that led us here. We didn't start having problems until we married, and then it was like you assumed I'd just be there no matter what. We need to learn from our mistakes in order to move forward."

He eased up, but when his wet palm covered her bare stomach, then slid up to cup her breast, Charlotte flinched and held her breath.

"Your reaction proves that no matter what stands between us, we love each other, Charlie."

Lily let out another squeal and flapped her hands on top of the water, pulling Charlotte from the realization that her husband's touch sent tingles up and down every nerve ending in her entire overheated body.

Charlotte adjusted Lily on her lap, knocking Anthony's hand off her breast. "Don't do this to me. Don't make me want things I can't have right now. I have so many feelings...I just can't."

He came to his full height, his eyes narrowing on hers.

"Don't do this to *you?* Don't make you feel? I'm finding it damn hard to stay in this house with you, knowing, in your eyes, I don't have the right to touch you. So don't tell me not to do this to you, Charlie. I love you and I'm damn well going to fight for you."

He stepped out of the pool, sending water sloshing over her and Lily. Charlotte hugged Lily and rocked on the step. Between the sexual tension sizzling between her and Anthony and the stress of adjusting to a new baby, she wasn't sure what emotion would envelop her next.

"Are you ready for your nap, honey?"

Charlotte scooped up Lily, kissed her on the nose and tried to stay positive. Arguing in front of the baby was not a good idea and certainly not a habit she intended to start.

"Maybe after your nap we can see about going for a walk," she told Lily, wrapping her in a hooded towel with a cat face.

Perhaps they could escape without Anthony seeing them. Because the last thing she needed was another confrontation like the one they'd just had. Charlotte feared the next time he touched her, bare skin to bare skin, she'd ignore every warning flare her heart shot out and take what she desperately wanted and he was so anxious to give.

Anthony cursed himself for losing it in front of Lily. Getting angry and frustrated certainly wasn't good for her, and it especially wasn't good for the marriage he so desperately wanted to save.

But dammit, he had feelings and he wasn't going to keep them to himself any longer. She'd always wanted him to be more open and he knew if there was any chance of their making this work, he had to be honest about everything.

He clenched his fist as he looked out the patio doors from his bedroom. When he'd slid a hand up her abdomen and over her breast, she'd sucked in her breath and asked him to stop.

Stop what? Stop loving her? Stop fighting for her? Not

likely, but he realized he had to go about getting his wife back in a different manner.

But first he needed to apologize. As much as he hated admitting that he was wrong, he knew he needed to show her he was man enough to own up to his mistakes.

Once Lily was in bed for the night, he'd show Charlotte how sorry he was. He knew exactly how to start making up for his recent actions.

Seven

"You ready for bed, sweetheart?"

Charlotte tugged the zipper up on the footed pajamas as Lily let out a tiny yawn. She had no clue where Anthony was, but he'd missed bath time. She wasn't going to beg him to help. He either wanted to or he didn't, and if he was so determined to show her how "dedicated" he was to their family, this was a poor way of going about it.

Charlotte turned on the gentle lullaby music that Lily had been falling asleep to. She picked up the sweet-smelling infant and held her to her chest. Before she knew it, she was swaying back and forth with Lily, humming to the tune, counting the steps in her head as she spun in wide, slow circles. A waltz with a baby, how precious.

"You always did like to dance."

Stunned, Charlotte turned at the sound of Anthony's voice. Oh, my. The sight of her husband in only his black boxer briefs never failed to render her speechless. After nearly a decade of marriage and knowing every inch of his body, Charlotte still found her husband to be irresistibly sexy and desirable.

And she knew if she had to walk away at the end of this, she'd never find anyone who made her heart beat wildly at just the sight of him or made her want him with just one look.

"We were getting ready for bed," she told him, somewhat embarrassed. For years she'd asked Anthony to take dance lessons with her, but that was just another thing that didn't fit into his schedule.

"Sorry I wasn't here for the bath. I was...busy," he told her, moving into the nursery. "I'll get her to sleep. Why don't you go down to the patio and wait for me. We need to talk."

Talk? Yes, they did. And this little reprieve would give her the time she needed to gather her courage and tamp her hormones down a notch...or five. She needed to tell him about the miscarriage last year and get some of this guilt off her chest.

If she truly wanted to see if this marriage would work, she had to be honest. But first she wanted to revel in the fact Anthony was helping so much and the fact that he seemed eager to do so. This was the father, husband she'd always wanted. This was the man who could make their marriage work.

"Her bottle is ready." Charlotte pointed to the small table beside the rocker.

Anthony came within inches and ran his fingertips up her bare forearms. Charlotte froze, her hands on the warm baby. But he did nothing more than get her nerves standing on end before he scooped up Lily, lifted her in the air and twirled her around.

"Come on, Lily Bug. What do you say to Uncle Anthony feeding you tonight? We seem to get along when I'm feeding you. Can I rock my girl?"

My girl.

Charlotte turned from the room, grabbing the extra monitor on her way, since she and Anthony would be outside. She couldn't stand in there, not with the image they were making.

Happy father playing with their baby. The intimacy of him wearing only his underwear and Charlotte in her cotton halter-style nightgown. They weren't that happy family who shared bedtimes and loving moments when the day was done. They weren't a laughing family, sharing a bond and depending on each other for everything.

Right now they were the epitome of broken, and Charlotte had to keep that in mind if Anthony decided he was done playing house and his work took top priority again. But she still held out hope that he would see that family could and always should come before a job.

So he was putting Lily to bed and was doing so without her asking. She had no doubt that he was trying to make up for this afternoon. She knew him and she knew he didn't like raising his voice or getting angry. No, Anthony had always been the fun-loving, good-time guy. To bare his emotions like that was new, and Charlotte figured he'd shocked himself and now wasn't sure how to deal with it.

She glanced back into the room one more time and her heart clenched at the sight of Anthony's strong arm cradling Lily, the way his broad shoulders hid the majority of the rocking chair. The soft words he murmured to her as he fed her a bottle.

How would he take the news of the miscarriage? Would he be angry at her for keeping the secret? Would he be sad at the loss?

Needing another barrier in this battle she waged with herself, Charlotte went to her room to grab her matching silk robe. Too bad she didn't own one of those big, thick, down-to-the-ankle terry-cloth numbers. That would be a much better coat of armor.

She headed down the stairs toward the living room. But her breath caught when she looked out through the French doors and onto the patio, which basked in the glow of the moonlight. The gentle light slanted through the tall evergreens. But it wasn't Mother Nature's beauty that had her stopping in her tracks. It was the bundle of blue hydrangeas in a short, etched glass vase and the beautifully wrapped present sitting beside the bouquet.

Quickly she crossed the room and went out into the warm night air, anxious to see what he'd done. Charlotte eased over to the table and fingered the pink silk ribbon that covered the thick, white, embossed paper.

Anthony was a master at charm and seduction. How else did she explain why she'd stayed married to the man this long? Yes, she loved him, but it was that always-present appeal and temptation that kept her sticking through tough times. Pretty words and affection tended to cloud her judgment.

Easing down onto the chaise beside the table, she stretched out and stared at the night sky. She would not be bought. Material things meant nothing to her if the gift didn't come from the heart and if the gift was just a ploy.

So here she sat, staring at the twinkling stars and the full moon just beyond the tall evergreen trees rising from the mountains surrounding Lake Tahoe. For the past few minutes she'd listened to the subtle tone of Anthony's voice as he talked to his niece.

"You have a very special lady in your life, Lily Bug."

Staring at the monitor, Charlotte shifted in her seat, uncomfortable that she was intruding on what he assumed was a private moment.

"We both love you and no matter what happens between me and your aunt Charlie, we want you to know that. I'll admit, this is all so new and scary. I hope I'm doing this right."

That made two of them, she thought. The idea of being Lily's guardian was an honor, but in reality she was scared to death. Yes, she'd interacted with hundreds of children through her volunteer work at the hospital, but when a child was your sole responsibility, that made being the caregiver so much different.

Charlotte listened to the silence, then the shuffling as Anthony placed the baby in the crib. Within a couple minutes he'd be out here and they'd be all alone. Alone with the ambience of romantic moonlight. Alone with the sexual tension. Alone with her out-of-control hormones, sitting next to her husband... whom she refused to touch. And alone with this secret he deserved to know first.

He also wanted to talk about something, so she'd hear him out.

Footfalls shuffled along the concrete behind her and Charlotte took a deep breath, bracing herself for the next several life-altering moments.

"I looked for the monitor to bring, but I see you have it." He took a seat in the chaise on the opposite side of the small table between them. "You were listening."

"Yes."

"Glad I didn't open up about all my secrets to Lily."

Charlotte smiled, just as he'd intended her to, she knew. "Good thing."

He stared at her and Charlotte shifted her gaze to the moon's mirrored reflection on the lake. "Beautiful night."

"Beautiful," he whispered, still keeping his eyes on her. "Never anything more so."

"Why the present?" she asked, still not looking his way.

"Why not? It's something you'll like and I wanted to show you how much I appreciate all you're doing with Lily. I couldn't do this without you."

She threw him a glance, praying her strength held out. "I hope you're not just trying to get me back into bed."

Anthony's soft chuckle washed over her, sending even more goose bumps dancing over her skin. "You don't honestly think you can go the whole time we're here and not make love to me, do you, Charlie? Be realistic. I understand you don't want me to try to seduce you, but we both know I can. And I will. But first I want to earn back your love."

Earn back her love. He'd never mentioned or even hinted at this before. Hope flourished even more within her, now that he was tapping into her inner emotions in ways she'd never expected. Thank God he cared enough, wanted her enough.

"If I end up sleeping with you, it still changes nothing." Okay, so she had to say that as a buffer in case she actually did lose her mind and let her hormones take over. And since when did she put a disclaimer on sex? "I'm still not making any guarantees at the end of the ninety days."

"What if I've become the man you want, the man you deserve? Then what?" he asked.

Charlotte sat up in the chaise, swung her feet to the warm concrete and looked at her husband, all deliciously spread out on the other chair. "If that happens, I'll be the first to fight for this marriage. But you're putting a lot on yourself to fix years of problems in a few months. I don't want you to think I wouldn't help out with Lily. Is that what you're afraid of?"

In a flash, he was on his feet, wrapping his strong hands around her arms and pulling her up and against him. "You think I'm worried about making sure I get my weekends and holidays with Lily? I want my wife. *My. Wife.* I wanted you before Lily came onto the scene. And damn if I'm not taking back what I want."

His lips crushed hers as his fingers roughly shoved her robe down her arms and tugged at the tie behind her neck. The top of her nightgown fell away, but caught between their bodies. Charlotte didn't resist. Who was she kidding? He was right. They couldn't cohabit and not give in to their desire.

"You don't know how I've missed touching you, Charlie. You have no idea." His mouth met hers briefly. "I swore I wouldn't make love to you until I knew you were in this with your heart, but you have no idea how much I need you."

Oh, she had a pretty good clue. She craved him like air in her lungs. But how could her body betray her when she was still so torn about where their relationship stood? Wanting him was never, ever a problem. Keeping her emotions in check certainly was.

She arched into him as he peeled the rest of her gown away, leaving it to slide down her body and puddle at her bare feet. She groaned, stretching her body as he made love to her breasts. She'd always been sensitive there and now that she was pregnant, every touch sent her nerve endings dancing.

Pregnant. She needed to tell him about the previous miscarriage. Isn't that what she'd come out here to do?

"You're always so responsive," he murmured as he moved to the other breast. "So sexy."

She would talk later. Right now she needed him, ached for him.

Charlotte reached down, sliding her fingertips between his taut abdomen and the elastic of his boxer briefs. He brushed her hands aside and yanked his boxers down.

And sweet mercy, was there anything sexier than a man offering himself to you while standing gloriously naked with the glow from moonlight kissing his bronzed, muscular skin?

Was she actually doing this? Making love to her husband out in the open when she'd sworn she would talk first?

Yes, she was, and she was going to enjoy every minute of pleasure he gave her.

And Anthony knew how to pleasure.

He lifted her up and Charlotte wrapped her legs around his waist.

"You taste so good," he murmured against her lips as he carried her toward the oversized outdoor sofa. "I need you, Charlie. Need this."

"Me, too," she conceded. No point in denying that she wanted him, craved the feel of his body against hers. God, she'd missed his tender touches.

The feel of him between her legs had her moaning, shifting restlessly, silently pleading for more, knowing he'd draw this out and only make her ache longer.

Without breaking the kiss, he laid her on the soft cushions. Both hands trailed up her bare thighs until he found the elastic of her panties. He jerked them down and settled between her legs. Charlotte lifted her hips, locking her ankles around his back.

"Don't make me wait," she begged. "I can't."

Without a word, he cupped one breast, rubbing his thumb back and forth over her puckered nipple. At the same time his other talented hand roamed all over her heated, aching body. Fingertips slid up her inner thigh, parting her until she cried out with anticipation.

She didn't have to beg or wait; he slid his fingers into her slowly, then retreated.

"Anthony," she cried.

"Believe me, I'm in just as much of a hurry."

He rose to his knees, shifting to ease her legs wider.

Then before she could even let out another moan of frustration, they were connected.

It was always like this. Always that split second where everything between them was perfect. Blissfully and utterly… perfect.

As they moved together, Charlotte dug her fingers into his thick biceps as he leaned down to lavish kisses on her breasts again.

Anthony had never been a selfish lover. This was always the one area in which he most certainly put her needs first. Maybe that's why they always ended up naked.

"Open your eyes, Charlie."

She looked up, afraid of what he'd see in her eyes, afraid of what would be staring back at her.

And there it was. Beneath the sheen of perspiration over his brow, desire and love looked back at her.

She closed her eyes again, arching into him on the brink of release, yet not wanting this moment to end.

"That's it, baby," he urged. "Just let go."

That's all it took and Charlotte felt the bubbling anticipation burst as her body tightened, a cry escaping her lips seconds before he captured them.

His tongue darted in and out, mimicking their lovemaking. Within seconds Anthony stiffened and moaned against her lips.

She held on to his body until they both stopped trembling. And then reality set in.

"Don't," he told her, resting his forehead on hers. "Don't start thinking."

"How can I not?" she whispered.

He lifted his head and looked down at her. "Can't we just enjoy this moment? Can we save the regret speech for tomorrow?"

They were still joined in the most intimate way, his eyes were pleading and her body was still humming with delight. What else could she say but "Sure."

Tomorrow, she vowed. Tomorrow she'd open up about the miscarriage. If she truly wanted him to devote himself to this marriage, then she had to expect the same of herself.

Eight

Anthony was attempting to feed Lily when Charlotte came down the stairs the next morning. She hadn't spent the night in his bed as he'd hoped, but she had lain with him outside until well after midnight. And that was hours after they'd made love.

He'd take that monumental victory and add it to the others he'd accumulated. Eventually, she would be back where she belonged and they could move forward together as a family.

He never thought he'd enjoy being a father as much as he had this past week with Lily. Work had always been his excuse whenever Charlotte had mentioned children…but, in all honesty, he'd been terrified of being a dad. He'd had a wonderful childhood, but for some reason the thought of a child depending on him had always had him finding excuses to avoid the unknown.

"I didn't hear her wake," Charlotte told him. "I'm sorry she disturbed you."

He studied her face, her shaky hands. "You okay? You look a bit pale."

She brushed a hand through her bed-wrestled hair. "Oh, I was up late finishing some emails for the dedication of the new wing at the hospital. I'm just a little tired."

Not fully buying her story, he paused with the spoon in the rice cereal. But when the silence stretched out, he realized that she wasn't going to comment further.

"I took the monitor from your room this morning so you could rest. I told Lily Bug you needed to sleep because you had a late night."

A smile tugged at the corners of her mouth, then disappeared. "Thank you for the present. I just opened it this morning."

Placing another bite in Lily's mouth, he smiled. "There are no strings attached to it, Charlie. You enjoy art and I saw the charcoal set and thought you might want to make some pictures for Lily. Maybe add some more of your art here, as you have back in L.A."

Her shoulders sagged a little, her lids lowered. "I just don't know what to think anymore when you give me a gift for no reason."

He shrugged. "I didn't mean for it to be a bribe or anything other than my gratitude for all you've done and are doing."

"You knew exactly what I'd like."

He nodded. "We'll be up here two full weeks. I thought Lily and I could give you some time to yourself every now and then. I think she's getting more used to being around a man."

Charlotte crossed the island and laid a hand on his bare shoulder. "This means a lot to me. Thank you."

The look in her eyes, the joyful tone in her voice, told him he should've done more from-the-heart gestures in the past instead of just assuming she'd like another facial or spa appointment.

A glob of rice landed on his cheek as he was grinning like a loon up at Charlotte.

"Lily!"

Charlotte laughed as Lily squealed and Anthony couldn't

help but laugh, too. This is what he wanted. Laughter, playfulness. But would Charlotte take this moment, grab hold of it and join him in forging the family she'd always dreamed of, or would she shut it out for fear she'd get her heart broken again?

Knowing his wife, she'd erect that wall back up around her heart again. But he was used to a challenge. He hadn't made it to the top in Hollywood by sitting back and not taking chances and facing them head-on.

He'd take that wall she kept building around herself and knock the damn thing down. Then he'd show her how they were going to live happily ever after with Lily and a life full of dreams and love.

He couldn't change his past, but he could sure as hell get control of his future.

"You look beautiful," he told her. Immediately, he wished he hadn't said anything. Why couldn't he just let the moment be?

Her smile vanished, her eyes bored into his.

"I'm sorry," he told her. "It's just when you laugh like that, your whole face lights up and I…well, I've missed seeing that."

She took a sip of her juice and didn't respond. An uncomfortable silence settled around them. Had he been so stingy with his compliments over the years that one had her unsure of how to respond?

"What do you say we go shopping today?" he suggested, trying to break some tension.

"Shopping? You hate to shop."

He smiled and shrugged, spooning up another bite of rice. "Not with my two favorite girls, I don't. Besides, we can get Lily some pool toys and we can grab some lunch at that little café you love."

Charlotte was silent for a moment and Anthony feared she'd say no.

Please, Charlie. Take the olive branch.

Ironic—he was afraid his own wife would turn him down for a date. Could he be more pathetic?

"I'd love to," she told him. "Let me grab a shower. Just bring her on up when you're done and I'll get her ready."

Once Charlotte was gone, Anthony put down the spoon, grabbed one of Lily's pudgy hands and mocked a high five.

"Score one for the home team."

"I seriously don't think Lily needed this many pool toys," Charlotte exclaimed as she watched Anthony blow up the last of ten toys. "She's only one kid and we're just here for twelve more days."

He tossed the inflatable elephant into the pool to lazily float around with the others. "What if she gets bored with one? She needs options."

"I hope you get this spoiling out of your system." She laughed.

He stared at her, making her aware they were once again out here alone while Lily took her nap. "Are you feeling okay? You weren't this morning, but your coloring looks better now."

Warmth spread through her at his sincerity. "I'm fine. But I do need to talk to you now that we're alone."

"Something's bothering you."

She nodded. "Yes. I've kept something from you for a while. A year actually."

Anthony placed his hands on his narrow hips. "A year?"

There was no room for guilt now, only the truth. She walked over to a chaise and took a seat. When Anthony sat on the end of the chair, she adjusted her feet to give him more room.

"I had a miscarriage," she told him. "Last year when you were in Belize filming."

He sat up a little straighter, eyes wide. "A miscarriage? I didn't even know you'd been pregnant."

"I didn't know either until a few days after you'd left. I took a test and it was positive." She remembered the excitement, the joy of seeing those two pink lines. "I couldn't wait until you got home. I didn't want to tell you over the phone so I planned a surprise. I bought this silly little T-shirt that said #1 Dad."

Tears welled in her eyes and Anthony rubbed her bare leg. "My God, Charlie. How far along were you when you miscarried?"

"Seven weeks." She wiped her eyes, trying to force out the pain of the previous loss. "I miscarried a week before you came home. I only knew I was pregnant for a couple weeks, but certainly long enough to plan in my head. I had the nursery decorated, I had us on playdates at the park and with other parents. But one morning I woke up to serious cramping and I knew something was wrong."

Anthony stared at her, his hand still on her leg. He didn't speak and she could only imagine the anger he held now. She'd lied to him, taken an important part of their marriage and kept it hidden.

"Why are you telling me now?" he asked. "You could've kept it to yourself your whole life and I never would've known."

"You're right," she agreed. "But I see that you're trying to work on this marriage and I can't let this lie hover between us. You deserved to know." Just like he deserved to know about the baby she was carrying, but she needed to take this one step at a time.

Anthony eased closer, moving her legs up over his lap. "You were angry that I wasn't there."

Charlotte bit her lip, forcing the rest of her tears back as she nodded. "Yes," she whispered.

He reached out, cupped her face and looked into her eyes. "To say I'm sorry is really inadequate now. I'm furious, though."

Charlotte closed her eyes for a moment then looked back into his. "I know. I knew when I told you that you'd be angry at me."

"At you?" he asked. "Why the hell should I be angry with you? You discovered a miracle and were excited to tell me and

I wasn't there. Nor was I there when you had to suffer the loss and mourn on your own. My God, Charlie, how could you ever think I'd be angry at you when you've obviously been through hell…in private, I might add."

"You're upset with yourself?"

Charlotte eased back onto the cushions, relieved he didn't flat-out hate her or worse…blame her for the loss.

He came to his feet, shoved his hands in his pockets and shook his head. "We both know I haven't been there for you and this just proves it. I was so out of tune with your feelings that I didn't even pick up on your sadness when I returned. I don't recall anything about that time that makes me think you were upset."

She slid her feet over the side of the chair and stood, as well. "I cried in private. I was angry that you weren't there so I kept it all to myself. To be honest, I didn't feel you deserved to know about the baby because you hadn't been there when I needed you."

Anthony's face crumbled, he looked down to the stone patio and sighed. "Have I ever been?" he asked, voice thick with emotion.

Charlotte had never, ever seen Anthony upset. He hadn't cried for his sister, at least in her presence, but here he stood obviously upset that she'd faced the miscarriage alone and he hadn't been there to help her through.

"When we first got married you were," she told him, crossing her arms over her sundress. "We were both different people then."

Anthony turned, walked toward the pool and kicked off his flip-flops. He sank to the edge and let his feet dangle in the water. Charlotte followed him, wondering what thoughts were swirling around in his mind. He was talking. More and more each day he talked to her about important things in life.

She sat beside him, letting her own legs dangle in the water.

"I want to be the husband and father this family needs to

survive," he told her, kicking a pool toy as it floated by. "I never want you to feel that you have to keep something from me or that you have to do everything on your own. I want you to trust me again, to trust the team that we can be."

"That's all I've ever wanted," she agreed. "I just need time. I want this to work and I don't want to rush into another chapter of our lives without really thinking about how we can fix the past."

Anthony rested his hands on his knees and nodded. "I visited Mia and Bronson right before Rachel passed. They were just home from the hospital with baby Bella. They seemed so happy, so in love. For once in my life, I was actually jealous of what Bronson had."

Intrigued at his choice of words, Charlotte smiled at the image of Mia and Bronson. "They seem so happy together. I hope they don't fall prey to the Hollywood hype and lose sight of what's important."

Anthony glanced up at her. "The way we did?"

She hadn't meant to say that, hadn't meant to make this another vulnerable moment for either of them. They'd had a good day and she wanted to relish it.

But her emotions had other plans. And obviously her subconscious wanted to dive into another layer of emotional angst.

"Yeah." She sat beside him and toed a floating duck that drifted by her dangling feet. "The way we did."

"We'll get through this," he told her, resting a hand on her bare thigh where her sundress had slid up. "If I learned anything this past year with finding the Danes and losing Rachel, I know how important family is, Charlie. I need you. We have so much at stake now."

Did that mean before, when only she was "at stake," their marriage wasn't worth fighting for? She wasn't going to ask; she didn't want to hear the answer. On the one hand she was thrilled that he was fighting for these kids—even if he didn't know about one of them yet—it was the most emotion she'd ever seen him show outside of business. But, on the other hand, she wished he'd realized he wanted to really fight for their marriage before fate gave them no other choice.

Yes, he'd said he hadn't wanted to lose her, but he hadn't done anything to keep her. The problem was, he'd never thought she'd leave. He'd never said so, but she knew that's what had been going through his mind. He thought she'd stay as long as he plied her with the latest sporty car, a mansion fit for a queen and all the shopping trips and spa treatments she could handle.

But that wasn't her. She never had fit the mold of the "Hollywood wife." She could care less that Botox-obsessed women snubbed their pointy noses at the crow's feet around her eyes. And so what if she had ten pounds she needed to lose—and that was prepregnancy weight. She certainly wasn't going under the knife to have that "perfect body."

No, the illusion of perfection was so distorted in Hollywood, Charlotte never had the desire to even try to keep up with how society suggested she look.

Anthony had loved her once for the way she was. Perhaps that was it. Perhaps he wanted that slim, wrinkle-free, spray-tanned beauty. Maybe she'd let herself go in his eyes. Maybe she wasn't made-up enough or devoted enough to his work the way some Hollywood wives were.

"What are you thinking?" he asked.

She turned her head, raising a hand to block the setting sun from her eyes. "I'm wondering if we grew apart because you are Mr. Hollywood and I'm at the opposite end of the spectrum when it comes to being a hotshot's wife."

"What are you talking about?" he asked, jerking his attention toward her.

Charlotte shrugged. "I'm not asking for pity or a compliment, Anthony. I'm just stating that we live in an area where looks are everything and I don't measure up to the other Hollywood wives. I'd rather spend my time and money on helping those children at the hospital."

He hopped in the pool, clothes and all, and came to stand between her legs. "I don't want a fake, plastic woman, Charlie. I want a genuine wife who doesn't get swept up in that hype."

Shocked, she looked down at his cargo shorts, which were now plastered to his thick thighs, and his black polo shirt, which was halfway into the water and floating around his waist.

"Um…you jumped in with your clothes on."

Way to point out the obvious.

"Because I wanted to look you in the eye when I tell you if I wanted a collagen-filled, implanted wife, I'd have picked one out years ago. I don't like fake and my tastes haven't changed."

A shiver of arousal crept up her back, sending that tingling sensation all over her body. She didn't know how to respond to that. Didn't know what to say when he stood before her, gazing into her eyes with that desire she always found. But she wanted more than sex every time they were together. She was getting drawn back into his charms quicker than she meant to, but she couldn't deny her love.

"I need to get inside and check on Lily," she told him as she started to pull her legs from the water.

His hands landed on her bare thighs where her sundress had ridden up, holding her firmly in place. "Don't. We have the monitor."

Water trickled down her legs as his big, strong hands held her in place. Her heart beat a bit faster because she didn't know if he was going to pull her into the water with him or if he'd just lean in to kiss her.

And she had no doubt that Anthony's intentions were taking a direct path toward seduction and she was about to get run over along the way.

"This is a mistake," she whispered. "I know last night we couldn't help it, but I can't keep doing this."

His signature wicked smile spread across his face. "I'm not doing anything but standing here talking to my wife."

"You know exactly what you're doing." She smiled. "Don't torture yourself further by trying to grab on to a few moments of pleasure when the end result with us could be the same."

His smile disappeared as his hands slid up higher. "I intend to have more than a few moments of pleasure, Charlie. I intend to have years of it. With you. We were made for each other and you know it. I see how you look at me. I felt you come apart in my arms last night and I'm guessing it wouldn't take much for you to do it again right now."

He moved one hand up over her bare shoulder. "I know how you like your shoulders tickled just…like…this." His fingertip trailed down her collarbone to the swell of her breast just above the line of her strapless sundress. "If I dipped my finger in here, what would I find? Hmm?"

With both hands, he slid the top of her dress down, grazing the tips of her sensitive breasts, first with the material, then with the pads of his thumbs.

Instinctively, her body betrayed her as her back arched toward his feather-light touch.

Then suddenly, he was gone.

Charlotte opened her eyes to see Anthony moving up the steps and out of the pool. "What are you doing?"

Blocking the sun with his wide shoulders, he looked down to her. "As much as I want to make love to you, Charlie, I want you to come to me. I want to know that the next time we make love it will be because you want to be with me. Not for the moment, but for the lifetime I'm willing to give."

Nine

Sexually frustrated? Hell, yes, he was. But Anthony pulled on dry clothes, determined to stand his ground no matter what the cost. At this point what did he have to lose?

Trembling with an ache that only Charlotte could fill, he knew he'd made the right decision. She wanted him—that had never been the problem between them. Quite honestly, he was just coming to see what their problem truly was—lack of communication and keeping his marriage above everything else.

They needed to embrace the love they first shared, before Hollywood entered, before his career and before Lily brought them back together. He missed that love, wanted so desperately to get it back, only better this time.

Yes, sex was easy. It was the other stuff that came with love that made a marriage work—that push-pull of emotions. Which was why it was so hard to walk away from her when she'd been pushing those beautiful breasts against his hands. The glow from the afternoon sun had beat down on her, making her seem like the goddess he'd always known she was.

But he'd had to walk away. He couldn't make love to her again until she decided whether or not she could forgive him and give him another chance with this marriage.

God knew the last thing he deserved was forgiveness. She'd been pregnant and suffered a miscarriage. The void he'd had in his life was nothing compared to the anguish and loneliness she must've felt. He needed to be here for her, not just physically, but emotionally.

A miscarriage. How could she forgive him for not being there when she needed him most? How could he forgive himself?

They'd made a baby out of their love, and he'd never known. He'd been so self-absorbed and wrapped up in work that he hadn't noticed the pain his wife was going through.

He leaned forward at his desk in the study and braced his elbows on the shiny mahogany top. Perhaps the miscarriage was a sign that they weren't ready for children. He certainly hadn't been at the time. And even though Lily had only been in his life a short time, he treasured every single moment.

When he'd first discovered that he and Charlotte were the guardians, he'd been shocked and on the verge of weaseling out of this guardianship, but then reality set in and he knew his sister trusted him with this baby for a reason. She had faith in him, so he had to have faith in himself.

And, yes, he was new to this parenting gig, so he was bound to have slipups, but now that he'd had some hands-on experience, so to speak, he wasn't so terrified of messing up as he had been. He could and would excel at being a father. Being a director wasn't the only talent he held.

And perhaps Charlotte's miscarriage had also happened because God knew there was no way they could raise two kids. He needed to get used to being with Lily, and he was thankful they didn't have another child thrown into the mix.

One child was enough, especially since he was bending

over backward to make his wife see him as the husband she'd been needing.

Maybe, once they returned home, he would invite his mother for a weekend. Even though she lived less than an hour away, he'd like to have her close by for a few days. Maybe Victoria could come, too. Hopefully, that would help mold his two families together and help Charlotte adjust, make her feel that he was pulling her into his life even more, where she definitely belonged.

Eventually, he'd have Bronson, Mia and their new baby over. Their brotherly bond was a bit slower in coming. They were both still getting used to the fact that they were related. After years of loathing someone, it was hard to just accept that the same blood ran through his veins and he would probably be spending holidays around the same fancy family dining table.

But the buffer Olivia provided helped with Bronson, and maybe it would ease some of this tension with Charlotte and help her feel more like she belonged to a family. Each day he was on pins and needles, wondering if Charlotte was going to decide to cut the trip short and say she was finished. On the other hand, he prayed he'd wake one day and she'd be curled beside him, the way she used to be.

They'd taken a giant step today in their marriage. Charlotte had opened up about her miscarriage and, for once, Anthony comforted her, listened to her when she truly needed him.

Anthony ran a hand through his hair, wiped his face with his palms and forwarded several emails to his assistant to deal with. Nothing too pressing for him. Certainly nothing that couldn't wait until he returned home. And, he realized, confident on the direction he and Charlie were headed, nearly everything work-related could wait. Not all emails and phone calls were emergencies, as he'd once thought. No, the emergency was keeping his wife. Period.

He sat back in his leather chair and smiled. He'd never let work take a backseat to his personal life before. In all honesty, it felt damn good to know he was taking care of and worrying about what was most important at this point. But his assistant was paid handsomely for a reason. The only thing that could bring him back to work right now was if Bronson or Olivia came to him with their latest project.

He wanted to discuss the film depicting Olivia's life and he was champing at the bit for Bronson to ask him to be the director, but he also had to tread carefully. He wanted Charlotte to be part of his decision making, and he only hoped when the time came she would support his directing the film of his mother's life.

Olivia had all but told him the project was his; he just wanted confirmation from Bronson. The fact that they were brothers now really put a new spin on the way they viewed each other.

And the press had had a field day with that bit of juicy family gossip. No word of the rivalry between the men was mentioned in the press release the family had put out, but all the media outlets were speculating and waiting to see just what would happen with the next film either man chose. Would they bury the hatchet and work together or would they continue to avoid each other, as they had the past several years?

Anthony was all for putting the past behind them and moving on. After all, his previous assistant had married the man, so he had to have some redeeming qualities. And Anthony couldn't deny that Bronson was the best producer in the industry.

He'd worked with some of the best writers in the industry and even dabbled at writing himself, so why the hell couldn't he write a script for his life? Why couldn't he figure out some way to make this work out for the best? Granted, not all his movies ended happily ever after, with the hero saving the heroine, riding off into the sunset. But dammit, that didn't mean his life couldn't go that way.

So maybe he was getting soft, but he wanted to be able to

ride to the rescue of Charlotte. He wanted to be that one person she turned to when she needed to feel secure and loved.

Unfortunately, he hadn't been that person for her.

From here on out, he'd show her that he could put her ahead of his work and any other aspect of his life. Which was all the more reason to include her in the decision making about this upcoming film he hoped to direct.

No doubt she'd felt pushed behind when he'd discovered he was the son of the Grand Dane of Hollywood. Especially when Charlotte wasn't in love with the whole Hollywood scene anyway.

But he wanted Charlotte to feel as if she were part of his new family, and he wanted to start moving forward with both of them. He knew she hadn't had the most loving childhood or doting family, and here he'd had two in his lifetime. He wanted to show her the love of a family, to show her how that bond could connect you forever. He wanted that bond as a bedrock of their marriage, and what better way than to envelop her in the love of his birth family?

No time like the present.

He picked up his phone and dialed Olivia's personal line.

"Anthony, darling," she answered on the first ring. "How are you?"

He smiled. How could he not with a warm greeting like that?

"I'm good. I was wondering if you and Victoria would like to come to visit me and Charlotte when we get home. You can play with Lily," he taunted, knowing there wasn't a woman alive who wouldn't want to spend time with a baby she could spoil then return to the parents. "I'd like you to actually spend the weekend with us to get to know Charlotte and Lily. I think we could all use some family time."

"I'd love to," she told him. "Victoria is in the midst of creating wedding dress designs for her friend Prince Alexander's fiancée, but I'm sure she'd love some baby time. I can ask her, but don't hold your breath. That girl works herself to death designing and sewing all those lavish gowns."

"And you're very proud."

Olivia's sweet laughter filtered through the phone. "That I am, Anthony. But even if Victoria cannot come, I'll certainly be there. There's nothing I'd love more than to spend time with my son, his wife and a beautiful baby. How are you doing, though, really?"

He came to his feet, shoved a hand in the pocket of his khaki shorts and glanced out the window behind his desk. From here he could see Charlotte walking around the pool picking up all the toys and putting them in the pool house.

"I'm okay," he answered after a moment, hoping to keep his emotions from seeping out.

That whole miscarriage revelation had left a raw, aching hole in his heart and he was determined now, more than ever, to give Charlotte all the love—and family—she needed. To make her realize she needed him and Lily.

"You don't have to be strong for me," Olivia told him. "You've just lost the only sister you've ever known, you're now raising her child and your marriage is a mess."

Anthony laughed. "You don't sugarcoat things, do you?"

"Why? That doesn't help solve the problem. Might as well face it head-on and deal with it." Olivia quieted for a moment, then spoke again. "Are you sure you want company when you get home?"

Just watching his wife stroll around the side of the pool in her little summer dress with the sun casting a glow on her tanned skin and glossy hair was making him insane with desire. "Trust me, we could use the buffer of another adult, and I think Charlotte has felt pushed aside with all the upheaval in my life lately. I want her to see that all of you are loving, and I want you to welcome her into the family so she can see she's not being shunted aside but becoming part of something even greater."

"She's lucky to have you," Olivia said. "It's not often a man will fight to keep his wife, especially in L.A. And I'd love to get to know her better. I'll call Victoria right now. One or both of us will be there next Friday evening."

"Perfect."

He hung up, feeling more confident that he'd made the right decision. Charlotte had mentioned more than once that she'd like to meet Olivia, but Anthony could tell by her hesitation that she feared Olivia would be a diva or snub her nose at Charlotte because she wasn't a typical Hollywood wife. And with the tension between them as it had been the few months before their separation, he just hadn't thought the timing was the best. But now he knew timing was everything and it was the perfect opportunity for Charlotte to feel those open, inviting arms of Olivia Dane.

Anthony only hoped that Charlotte accepted the love and worked with him on this marriage. He knew she'd tried to keep their marriage strong before. He just hoped he wasn't too late to win back her love and trust.

"Olivia is coming for a visit when we get back home. And maybe Victoria. You don't mind, do you?"

Charlotte zipped up the pink-and-white sleeper on Lily. "Not at all. I'd love to see them. I just hope…"

Anthony crossed his arms and leaned against the wall beside the changing table. "Hope what?"

"Nothing." She picked up the baby, kissed her on the nose and turned away. "Can you grab that bottle for me?"

"I'll put her to sleep tonight. You did it last night. This parenting is a joint effort, and I like doing it."

Charlotte settled into the rocker. "I don't mind doing it again. I love snuggling with a fresh-smelling baby."

Anthony handed over the bottle and laughed. "You don't like when she smells ripe? Is that why you called me up for nap time?"

"Hey, I can't help it if she decided to fill her diaper just before you walked into the room."

He laughed, showcasing those gray eyes she'd fallen in love with. "I think you two are plotting against me. I'm outnumbered."

Charlotte shrugged. "Yes, you are."

He squatted down in front of the chair and ran a hand over Lily's swirl of dark hair. "I don't mind. All that matters is that we're a family."

Charlotte closed her eyes and sighed. "Anthony, I can't promise…"

"I know," he told her, resting his hand on the arm she had curled around the baby. "But I'm learning just how important family is. Every day I think of calling Rachel, but I can't. She's gone. I want to secure my family and spend the rest of my life proving to all of you how much you mean to me and how much I love you."

Once they returned to Hollywood, to the scene of the crime, so to speak, would he get swept back into the world of glitz and glamour and push her aside once again? But things were moving in the right direction, and she would focus on the positive.

In his defense, though, she'd never opened up to him, never expressed her feelings and fears of always coming in last on his priority list. So how could he have known he needed to reevaluate his life? She had to take half the blame. She shouldn't have always assumed he knew how she was feeling.

"What are you thinking?"

Charlotte glanced up from where Lily's puckered little lips formed an O around the bottle. Anthony stared up at her, causing her heart to clench.

"This is all I've ever wanted. All I'd ever dreamed about and here it is. But at what cost? Rachel is gone, our marriage is falling apart, but I have a sweet baby in my arms and you professing how much you'll be there for me and love me until I die."

"Then why can't you just take this for what it is?" he asked. "Take what fate has handed us."

Tears pricked her eyes. "If moving forward were that easy I would. But there are years of hurt inside me, Anthony. I can't ignore that."

"Are you saying I can? I'm here for you, Charlie. You and Lily. I'm not going anywhere and, more than that, I'm sticking closer than I ever have. I know I'm going to have to earn back your trust, but I swear I'll always be there when you need me. My priorities are shifting back into the right order."

Charlotte gazed into his eyes, wanting to believe every word he said. Wanting *him* to believe them, too.

"I would've given you a baby at any time," she whispered. "I would've given you a family."

"I never thought I would be ready," he admitted, glancing down to Lily, then back to Charlotte. "I didn't know how this would change my life, our marriage. I guess I always had a fear of the unknown. That's no excuse, but I'm being honest."

Which she appreciated.

"And now?" she asked. "Are you ready now?"

"I love Lily as if she were my own."

He stared at her a moment longer, then came to his full height. He leaned over, kissed Lily on the head before moving his lips to land on Charlotte's cheek.

The whisper-soft touch had her rippling with delight and lowering her lids as if to savor the moment.

"We can talk after you lay her down," he whispered against her skin. "I'll be in our bedroom."

She didn't even bother correcting him. That spacious master bedroom overlooking the lake wasn't "their" room anymore, but arguing with him was pointless. He was dead set on getting this marriage back on track, and if he devoted as much time to making it work as he did to just talking about it, they'd certainly have no problem reconciling.

Is that what he wanted to discuss? Did he expect her to

remain in their Hollywood Hills home after the ninety days were up?

There was no way she could make any promises or plans that far ahead. She'd always been a planner, but there was so much uncertainty in her life right now. She hated not having that stability she'd grown so accustomed to.

He hadn't exactly answered her question—that didn't slip by her. Was he ready to be a fully devoted father, husband? Could he really balance that very fine line between career and personal life and be happy? Because as much as she wanted him to be a husband and father, she also didn't want him to be miserable.

There had to be a happy medium somewhere. They just had to find it.

In no time Lily was asleep. Charlotte sat her up for a minute or two to make sure the formula settled and wouldn't cause reflux. Quietly, she laid her down in the crib and smiled at the sleeping bundle. There was nothing more precious.

After closing the door, Charlotte took the bottle downstairs to the kitchen to rinse it in the sink. She went ahead and fully washed it, placing it in the drying rack because she needed the extra few minutes to gear up her strength to face her husband.

That was a low trick he'd pulled earlier in the pool, and she wasn't the least bit amused.

She dried her hands on the towel and headed back up the stairs to the master suite. Anthony wasn't in the room but out on the balcony. He'd left the doors open, and the soft, late summer breeze from the lake blew in the sheers.

The scene was set as if Anthony the director had worked one-on-one with Mother Nature to create the perfect setting to entice her. And like the moth drawn to the flame, Charlotte followed the gentle lake winds and stepped onto the balcony.

"I'm sorry if you're uncomfortable," he told her the second she came to stand beside him and rest her back against the concrete rail.

Okay, not what she'd expected to hear, but she'd see where he went with this.

"My original intention in having you here in Tahoe was to seduce you, to make you see what amazing chemistry we have so you couldn't walk away. But that was shallow and wrong. You need so much more. *We* need so much more than sex to make this work." He sighed and hung his head between his shoulders before looking back out into the night. "I didn't know how much before we came here."

Charlotte swallowed, lacing her fingers over her abdomen, moving her head to the side to allow the wind to blow her hair out of her face so she could focus on the man who was attempting to bare his soul. "But what do we have?"

With his forearms resting on the rail, he turned and looked up at her. "We have a broken past, but I hope we have a loving, solid future."

She took a deep breath before broaching the topic that had been a bone of contention with them for years. "Will you go to counseling with me?"

He bit the inside of his cheek. He knew she'd ask. What did it matter how many times a week they had sex? Did he leave the seat up or down? And did he ever do spontaneous things to surprise her?

That's how the first, and only, session had gone. But if answering private questions would help him keep his wife, he'd answer each one of them with pleasure.

"Charlie." He sighed. "I don't think—"

"Forget it." She held up a hand and let out a wry laugh. "I knew you wouldn't want to do it. I was hoping that since you decided to come here, to really spend time together and work things out, that you might work with me on this."

The hurt in her voice sent a shooting pain through him.

He wasn't going to lie to himself and pretend that he was ready to be put under the microscope again. He wanted time alone with his wife and he wanted to build this marriage from the ground up, if needed. Then they could speak to a counselor.

"Okay," he told her. "I'll do anything to keep you, Charlie. Anything. And if opening up and sharing everything will make this marriage stronger, then I'll do it. I actually have asked a few friends who they would recommend, and I have a couple names of reputable therapists."

The look on Charlotte's face was more than worth the embarrassment or discomfort he might experience by talking out his problems with a stranger. He wasn't lying when he said he'd do anything for her.

"Anthony, you don't know how much this means to me," she told him, then kissed him on the cheek.

A warm, hopeful peace settled over him, and Anthony prayed this was the track that they were supposed to be on.

Ten

"Good morning."

Charlotte rolled over, the satin sheets swishing around her bare legs, and squinted her eyes at the intruder.

"You slept a little late this morning, so Lily and I decided to surprise you."

Charlotte looked beyond the bright sun streaming into the guest bedroom at the man who juggled a baby on his left hip and held a small tray of food in his right hand. He set the tray down on her bedside table, then shifted Lily and smiled.

"Surprise," he said with a big, sexy grin. "We made your favorite breakfast."

To think just a week ago he'd been unable to even hold Lily without her crying, and here he'd managed to make breakfast with the little one in tow.

Intrigued, Charlotte peeked over and, sure enough, a plate full of French toast, complete with maple syrup and powdered sugar, stared back at her. A single red rose lay along the edge of the tray. He was changing. Each day he was becoming more and more the man she needed. And last night he'd not only agreed to therapy, he'd looked into it already.

They were moving forward and for the first time in longer than she could remember, they'd stayed up late and actually talked…with their clothes on. After she'd told him about the miscarriage, he'd been so genuinely concerned with her emotions, her feelings. She'd never seen that side of him before.

And now he stood before her looking so sexy with a goofy apron around his waist, a baby on his hip and a full-fledged smile on his face. Yeah, this was a level of love she hadn't experienced in a long time.

If only the tabloids could see Mr. Hotshot Director now.

"It smells great." She sat up in bed, adjusting her gown over her breasts. "What made you do this?"

Lily started reaching for Charlotte and Anthony sat her on the bed next to his wife. "I wanted to," he told her.

She glanced his way curiously, hoping he'd elaborate, but obviously the answer was that simple. He was working extra hard to showcase a new side. And she loved this new Mr. Mom angle. She only prayed he wouldn't tire of this life of family and domestic bliss.

"Thanks." Charlotte looked down at Lily and kissed her on the nose. "Thanks to you, too, Lily Bug."

"Do I get a kiss? I did all the cooking, after all."

She glanced up at him and rolled her eyes. "Is that why you did this? To get affection?"

His devious smile widened. "No, but I'll still take it."

Loving this sweet, playful side, Charlotte shrugged. "Let me see how it tastes first, then we'll see how much affection you deserve."

He leaned down close to her ear and whispered, "It's so good, you'll have to show me your thanks in private."

As he eased up, Charlotte caught his gaze roaming down the gap in her silk gown. Her nipples pebbled as his eyes grew darker with desire.

She loved this man. There was no off button to protect her from his charms and passion. She just wished she knew how exactly this would end up for her, for them. Could they really be this happy, fun-loving family once Anthony's career intervened again?

"I'll let you eat while it's hot." He scooped up Lily, who instantly began to cry. "Oh, come on," he begged. "We've made such progress."

Charlotte smiled. "Just leave her with me. We're fine."

Easing Lily back onto the bed amid a pile of pillows, Charlotte scooted over and took the tray Anthony handed her.

"Did she already have something to eat?" Charlotte asked.

"I fed her some apricots and she had half a bottle. I'll go clean up the kitchen because it seems she wasn't a fan of the apricots, and the mess under the high chair is horrendous. It looks like the jar of baby food was massacred."

Charlotte laughed. "Lily, you have to eat your fruits and veggies. You want to get big and strong like Uncle Anthony, don't you?"

Lily smiled and squealed, crawling over the pillows to reach for a piece of French toast.

"No, no," Charlotte said, moving the plate aside.

"I can take her," Anthony offered, reaching forward.

Charlotte held up a hand. "No, really. Go clean up the mess."

Anthony left her alone with her breakfast and a very chatty, grabby baby.

"How can I resist him?" Charlotte asked Lily. "He made breakfast in bed, fed you and is now cleaning. And he is making arrangements so I'm part of his new family. What woman wouldn't want that for a husband?"

Charlotte's tears spilled over and trickled down her cheeks. What woman indeed?

Charlotte was relaxing in the window seat, discreetly reading a book on pregnancy she'd packed for the trip and now had hidden inside a magazine when the doorbell rang.

Before she could get up, Anthony came sprinting through the kitchen, past the living area and yelled, "I got it."

Intrigued, Charlotte closed the magazine over the book and set it on the seat beside her, watching as Anthony opened the door. His body blocked the guest, so Charlotte got up and moved closer.

What was he up to? The way he'd run through the house made her realize he knew exactly who this mystery guest was. Another surprise?

She looked down at her leggings and off-the-shoulder T-shirt. Not exactly the perfect ensemble for company, but she'd felt a bit nauseous earlier and hadn't had the energy to put on anything fancier. Added to that, she was mentally exhausted from the phone calls and emails she'd worked on for the past few hours regarding the dedication of the new wing at the hospital. She'd forgotten how many details there were to finalize before such an extravagant event. The last major event she'd coordinated for the hospital took place nearly two years ago.

"Please come in," Anthony said to the guest after a minute of low murmuring.

"Good afternoon, Mrs. Price."

Charlotte smiled at Margaret, one of their loyal staff they used when they visited this property. "Hello, Margaret. Good to see you again."

The middle-aged lady smiled, darting a glance to Anthony. "Is Lily ready to go?"

Lily?

"What's going on?" Charlotte asked. "Where is Lily going?"

Like any obedient employee, Margaret kept her mouth shut and allowed Anthony to answer.

"Lily is going to spend the afternoon at the park playing with Margaret's grandchildren. I have a surprise for you."

Charlotte's mind went into overdrive. "But I'm not dressed and Lily's bag isn't packed."

"That's what I was doing while you were working on emails

for the hospital." Anthony smiled. "Lily woke from her nap and I kept her entertained with toys while I packed a bag for Margaret. Everything's all taken care of, so why don't you go put on a nice dress."

Stunned, Charlotte stood there before answering. "But I didn't pack a nice dress."

That signature grin that had gotten him through many interviews on the red carpet spread across his face. "I think you'll find something on your bed."

"But what about—"

Anthony stepped closer and placed a finger over her lips, sending sensations shooting through her that were completely inappropriate with Margaret standing so close.

"I've got it all taken care of," he whispered. "Go look on your bed."

Because his smile melted her heart, because his touch never failed to make her insides quiver like a teenager fresh in love, and because she wanted to see what he had in store for her, she smiled and all but ran to her room. Suddenly she wasn't exhausted, but anxious and excited.

How had he done this without her knowledge? She'd caught him in a private conversation earlier on the phone in the den, but she assumed it was business as usual. Even though he'd told her he wouldn't conduct business while on vacation, it wasn't as if he hadn't done that before. He'd also been gone for a couple hours earlier, but she'd been busy herself when she'd first laid Lily down for a nap and she hadn't questioned him.

Obviously, this is what he'd been so secretive about.

Charlotte froze in the doorway to her room. Spread across her bed was an emerald-green ball gown with thin straps at the top, an empire waist and a full, chiffon skirt. At the foot of the bed sat a pair of silver, strappy heels.

Were they going somewhere? Where on earth would you go wearing a ball gown in the late afternoon in Tahoe? They were surrounded by mountains, evergreens and water.

More than intrigued and even more excited to put on such a remarkable dress, Charlotte didn't waste time in changing. Anthony had obviously gone to great lengths to plan a surprise for her. She couldn't even begin to imagine what it would be, but she did allow herself to play Cinderella for a moment. What woman wouldn't?

Before she slid into the dress, Charlotte went into the restroom and pulled her hair up into a quick twist, securing it with some bobby pins. A little blush, mascara and pink lip gloss and she was presentable. At least she'd showered this morning while Lily was taking her first nap and when the nausea had worn off.

The silk, chiffon gown slid over her body and Charlotte turned one direction then the other in her floor-length mirror. The skirt swished about as she swayed and Charlotte couldn't stop the giddiness from bubbling out.

She smoothed the material over her abdomen and wondered how she'd look with a baby bump. Other than the occasional nausea, she loved being pregnant and now feeling like the belle of the ball was more excitement than she'd experienced in a long time. She eased one foot, then the other, into the heels and secured the straps around her ankles.

She wanted to tell Anthony about the baby. He was being so good with Lily, and deserved to know exactly what was going on so he could prepare himself. But that fear of a miscarriage kept niggling at her.

All the more reason to open up to Anthony. God forbid, if anything should happen, she'd need his support more than ever. And she knew he was a different man now than he'd been last year, when she'd kept the baby from him. Now he seemed to be devoted, ready to be the strong man she so needed.

Unable to stop from looking in the mirror one more time at the magnificent gown, Charlotte smiled. Could this marriage work? Could they get back what they'd once had? Anthony was obviously trying to please her, trying to go out of his way to make her happy. First the charcoals and then the way he wanted to learn how to do basic things for Lily and be a great father figure to her. And now this. She didn't care what lay ahead today—whatever it was came from his heart.

With the odds in their favor of making this marriage work now more than in the past, Charlotte headed back downstairs to see just what Anthony's plans were.

Though she still couldn't commit to anything beyond the ninety days, she hoped by then she'd have all the answers.

Eleven

When Charlotte came into the living area, Anthony had changed into a black dress shirt and black pants and was having a murmured conversation with a very handsome, very tall Latino man.

Not only that, the leather sofas and tables had been pushed to the outer walls to expose the entire hardwood floor of their spacious living area.

"Charlotte." Anthony turned as she entered the room, extending his hand toward her. "Come meet Rico. He's here to give us dance lessons."

Dance lessons?

Smiling, she turned her attention to their guest as she moved toward Anthony's outstretched hand. "Really?"

"I'm honored to be here," he told her with a thick Latino accent. "Mr. Price tells me it has been your dream to learn how to waltz. I am here to make that dream come true and show you some other basic dance steps. Dancing is the language of love. Yes?"

Anthony squeezed her hand. "Yes," he replied. "Where would you like us?"

Rico moved to the surround-sound entertainment area and turned on a slow, romantic ballad.

"First, I want to see how you hold her, Anthony."

Anthony turned toward her, winked and lifted one corner of his mouth. "My pleasure."

Oh, mercy. When he looked at her like that, held her in those strong, muscular arms, she didn't have a chance. She literally melted when he pulled her into his embrace and slid an arm around her waist.

"How's this?" he asked, never taking his gaze off her.

"Wonderful," she whispered.

He eyed her mouth. "I was asking Rico, but I'm glad to know you're comfortable."

"Perfect," Rico said, moving in behind Anthony. "I'm going to place my hands on your arms and guide you through the steps."

Rico reached his arms around Anthony's and began telling him how to move his feet, how to stay in the lead and how to take charge on the dance floor. After a few moves around the makeshift dance area, Rico stood off to the side and guided them without touching.

All his words registered with Charlotte, but the silk swishing around her bare legs, her body sliding against Anthony's and the way he never took his eyes off her made it hard to concentrate.

Anthony had planned this for her. Years ago she'd mentioned taking ballroom-dancing lessons with him, but he'd told her there was no way he'd let some leotard-wearing man teach him how to dance with his wife.

She'd dropped the subject after that, but he'd caught her dancing with Lily and obviously her wants overrode his dislikes. Another sign of progress. So here they were dancing, and Anthony was enjoying himself, if the bulge that brushed against her abdomen was any indication.

"I think you have that down," Rico said. "What do you say we move on to something hotter, sexier?"

Hotter and sexier? Anthony was already hot and Charlotte was sure as hell sexy in that emerald-green dress he'd chosen for her, knowing it would look amazing with her green eyes.

She'd worn green to one of his early premieres and he'd never forgotten how stunning she'd looked in the striking color.

He also hadn't forgotten her love of dance. She'd told him that she'd taken dance lessons as a kid until her parents couldn't afford it anymore. Then, when she'd suggested that they take them together, he'd had a near panic attack. There was no way he was interested in letting another man touch his wife to show her how to dance and be sexy. But when he'd seen the smile on her face as she danced with Lily, he knew he wanted to see more of that happiness. He wanted her to stay after the court date, not out of obligation but out of love.

He wished he'd taken her up on the lessons all those years ago when she'd asked. Her smile was absolutely beaming and the look in her eyes—the passion, desire and raw sex—was aimed directly at him.

Perfect. He didn't know how much longer he'd have to wait for her to finally invite herself into his bed, to share it with him again. He wasn't a patient man, but he knew once Charlotte decided she did indeed want him, the wait would be more than worth it, considering he'd have a lifetime with her.

Rico tilted his hips and did some crazy sashay move that no man should physically be allowed to do. Charlotte imitated him perfectly...too perfectly.

"You're a natural," Rico told her. He turned to Anthony. "Now you."

Anthony shook his head. "I'm not sure I can move like that."

"Stand facing your wife." He motioned Anthony to move

closer. "Now place your hands on her hips. Move them, Charlotte."

Anthony's palms burned from the fast swaying motions of Charlotte's very talented hips. When his gaze caught hers, he didn't miss the gleam in them. She knew she was driving him insane and he deserved every bit of this hell and so much more for hurting her.

"Now try to mimic her," Rico ordered.

Closing the minimal gap between them, Anthony had no problem with this dance. Her hips bumped against his, her chest mocked him as her nipples brushed against his thin shirt.

The art of having sex with clothes on should be the name of this dance.

"Shouldn't the man always lead?" Charlotte asked, keeping her eyes locked onto his.

"Oh, honey, he's leading," Rico retorted with a wave of his hand. "I knew he'd catch on quick. When a man looks at a woman the way your husband looks at you, the art of dancing is almost natural."

As grateful as Anthony was to Rico for having introduced them to this nearly erotic dance, Anthony wanted their instructor gone. Now. He wanted to enjoy the feel of his wife in his arms without a spectator. He wanted to peel this dress down her body and hear her beg him to take her to bed.

Charlotte kept her gaze on his and he knew if they were alone, they would've shed their clothes by now. Difficult as it may be, Anthony didn't want to make love again until Charlotte was ready to recommit to their marriage. But he wanted her to ache for him, to crave his touch the way he did hers... the way she used to.

He'd hurt her, that was obvious, but he felt they were making progress on rebuilding this marriage.

The revelation of her miscarriage had truly shocked him. Fatherhood had never been in the plan of his life, but now they had Lily. He wasn't sure he could handle more children or that their marriage was strong enough for more at this point. First he wanted to get used to being a father to Lily before he could even contemplate more…if he ever did.

But as Anthony stared at Charlotte's beauty, he couldn't help but wonder what a child they created would look like.

He splayed his hand across her back, easing her body even closer as he briefly touched his lips to hers.

"I think you two are going to burn up any dance floor."

Rico's proud tone didn't distract Anthony, not when Charlotte's eyes remained on his, never wavering.

When the song ended, Anthony leaned down to Charlotte's ear and whispered, "This needs to be a party of two."

Charlotte's heart clenched at Anthony's warm breath against her cheek, his promising words and how he'd held her and looked into her eyes as if she were the only woman he'd ever love and nothing else mattered.

Anthony moved to talk to Rico, the two men standing huddled on the other side of the room. Charlotte glanced to the wall clock and couldn't believe two hours had already passed. Dancing with Anthony, being in his arms, had been so amazing, so arousing, she'd lost all track of the time. And now Rico was leaving and who knew what Anthony had in mind?

Well, he was a man for one and she'd been married to him for many years, so she pretty well knew what was on his mind. Her body was so revved up after that fast, frenzied dance they'd just completed, her hormones were all over the place. She wanted this man, but that was just a physical response. On a deeper level, beyond the arousal and lust, she was falling for him all over again.

Once Anthony locked the door and turned to face her, Charlotte's heart beat so hard, so fast against her chest she feared he'd hear it. Like a panther stalking its prey, he moved slowly over the hardwood floors. One click after another of his shoes sounded until he stood directly in front of her with barely a brush of light between them.

"Dance with me," he told her, wrapping his arms around her and drawing her even closer.

Those hard plains of his body never got old. The power in his embrace, the fresh, masculine aroma that she associated only with Anthony never failed to make her knees weak and the female in her stand at attention, ready for whatever he wanted to give her.

But this was still fantasy. Yes, he'd done this amazing act for her, but she had to prepare herself: What if he decided family life wasn't for him? They were both so new to this. She only prayed that when the newness wore off he'd still find this personal side of his life appealing.

If she wanted to keep the marriage alive, she needed to come clean about the baby. Now that she'd told him about her miscarriage, she knew that even if the worst happened again, Anthony would be there for her.

"Rico turned the music off."

Charlotte hated stating the obvious, but she was a tad nervous and didn't know if she should talk to lighten the intense mood or remain quiet.

"You're shaking," he told her, ignoring her comment. "I'm flattered."

Charlotte laughed. "I'm cold."

Anthony ran a fingertip over her bare shoulder and down her arm. "Funny, you didn't have any gooseflesh until I touched you. If anything, I'd say you're hot."

"Anthony." She grasped his biceps, stopping the dance, and stared into his eyes. "I can't go any further until you know something."

"Will it take long? Because I'm dying to taste your lips again."

She gave a gentle squeeze. "I'm serious. And you may want to sit down."

"Charlotte, you're worrying me. What's wrong?"

He remained standing, so she held on to his arms, more of a brace for herself.

"I've seen how you've progressed with Lily," she told him, tamping down her nerves and fear. "You treat her like your own."

"That's the point of being a guardian, right? To make the child like your own." The corners of his mouth tipped up. "Besides, she's impossible not to love."

She knew all this, but hearing him say it out loud went a long way toward giving her the courage to say the next few words.

"I'm pregnant."

Anthony stared at Charlotte, his eyes instinctively darting down to her stomach. "Pregnant?"

He glanced back up to see her chewing on her bottom lip. "I'm almost six weeks now."

He raked a hand through his hair and blew out a breath. A baby? *Another* baby?

"I know you have a million thoughts going through your head," she told him, stepping forward to take his hand. "But we need to discuss what this means for us. I have to be honest. I'm scared, Anthony. I need you."

Anthony looked into his beautiful wife's face, humbled that she was seeing him now as her hero, her rock of support.

He brought their joined hands up to his lips and kissed her fingers. "Are you scared because of where we are in the marriage and with Lily or are you scared of another miscarriage?"

"Both. I love Lily, I love you and I love this baby." She closed her eyes and whispered, "I almost feel like I can't have it all. Like I need to choose what's most important and pray to keep it instead of being greedy and praying for all three."

Anthony swallowed any fear of another baby in his life. He couldn't focus on his own insecurities; he had to be strong for Charlotte. Unlike last time when he'd left her to deal with the hurt and loss alone. She was coming back to him, to their marriage. He only hoped he could be the father and husband she needed.

"You don't have to pick which one to pray for," he told her, bringing his hands up to frame her face. "I'm not going anywhere, especially now. My God, Charlie. We're having a baby. I love you, I want you to know that. You won't be going through anything else alone, especially this. Are you excited?"

A beautiful wide grin spread across her face. "I've always wanted babies. Before we had problems, I wanted your babies and I wanted to see you with them. To see how you were as a father. You're so amazing with Lily that I just know you'll be a great dad."

"So this happened when I came to visit you and we ended up not talking at all." Charlotte nodded. Anthony reached down, palmed her still-flat belly. "How long have you known?"

"Almost a week," she told him. "I didn't want to say anything until I saw where we stood and I just worry something will happen."

The silk of her dress bunched in his hand. "Nothing will happen. Do you hear me? We are going to be a family. We may have things to work on, but we will. And by the time this baby gets here, we will be so ready to love it. Lily will be a great big sister."

"I wanted you to be happy." She leaned forward, kissed his lips. "I wanted you to feel love for this baby already, as I do."

"How could I not? I'm so in love with the baby's mother."

Surges of excitement, arousal and pure, raw need coursed through her at his words, his touch. Anthony's gaze dropped to her mouth and Charlotte stepped toward him, unable to take another second without feeling a closer, deeper bond. This was still her husband, the father of her baby, and she wanted him.

He kept his hands on her face, but quickly took control of the kiss. His hips shifted against hers and there was no question as to how turned on he was. Good, because she was about ready to explode after that two-hour bout of foreplay.

Anthony backed her up until she felt the warm glass of the patio doors at her back. The sun streamed in around them and she'd love nothing more than to have him take her here with the lake at her back. She'd always had a bit of a reckless abandon when it came to making love, and now, after his emotional reaction to her revelation of the baby, she didn't care about finding a bed or even using the couch that had been shoved aside to make room for the dance floor. She wanted Anthony. Now. She wanted that passion they'd always had to go to another, more intimate level.

His hands cupped her bare shoulders as he broke off the kiss. "Tell me this is more than just desire."

Charlotte stared up at him. "What?"

"I need to know that you want me, this marriage. I don't want a commitment for the next few minutes. I want the rest of our lives."

Charlotte stared at him. Tears clogged her throat and all she could do was give in to the euphoria of the moment. The happiness, the intensity of their desire coalesced and felt like it had exploded inside her.

"Anthony, I want you. This. I will give us another chance."

For the beat of a heart, he studied her face before taking her mouth once again and going on to show her just how much he wanted her, too.

Twelve

"I have another surprise for you."

Charlotte glanced up from the antique wooden high chair where she was feeding Lily. If his surprise was anything like the previous day of erotic dancing and then making love, she wasn't sure her nerves could handle it.

"What's the surprise?" she asked, scooping another spoonful of puréed carrots from the jar.

That cocky grin that had melted her heart at their first meeting spread across his handsome face. "It wouldn't be much of a surprise if I told you."

Which meant she should prepare herself for anything.... She couldn't wait.

"Is Lily coming with us?" she asked, pretending her heart hadn't picked up the pace from the anticipation of the unknown.

"Yes, she is."

Well, that knocked wild sex on the beach out.

He leaned down, kissed her on the forehead. "How are you feeling?"

"Not too bad. A little dizziness when I first got up, but it passed."

She loved the feeling that swept over her as his caring, protective side emerged. That ball of nerves had vanished, leaving her thankful she'd opened up about the pregnancies—both of them. Now they could have a clean slate to work with and start this marriage on a stronger, more solid foundation.

"Can you both be ready in an hour?" he asked.

Just then, Lily spit up carrots all over Charlotte's face. Through the gooey mess, Charlotte eyed the baby, who was clapping and giggling, then Anthony, who had jumped back fast enough to avoid the spray of liquid veggies.

"We can try," she laughed, wiping her face.

Yesterday's surprise had been all about letting Charlotte see his softer, more compassionate side—just how committed he was to this marriage. Little had he known she had a surprise of her own: her pregnancy.

God, a baby. He'd been utterly caught off guard, so stunned he'd only wanted to feel closer to her, to connect in a familiar, comforting way.

But after they'd made love and she'd spent the night in his bed, where she belonged, he'd lain awake most of the night looking at the moonlight slanting across the ceiling.

How the hell was he going to make this work? He was just getting his wife back, trying to do what was right for Lily, mourn for Rachel, get to know his new family. And now he was going to be a father.

He'd never seen Charlotte so worried, yet so excited. The light in her eyes as she'd told him about the baby was something he wished he'd see more often. She was going to be a wonderful mother.... He only hoped, prayed, he could be the man he needed to be to all the people who needed him.

Most important, though, he needed to be a supportive, loving husband and father. If Charlotte leaving him taught him anything, it was that even with work in his life, there was still a void without the one woman he loved with every breath in his body.

And as intense and emotional as yesterday had been, today he wanted everything to be about them as a family, a unit. They were in Tahoe, where the lake glistened from the glorious sunshine and the century-old evergreens protected the land like a fortress. He wanted to enjoy the simpler things in life and he wanted to do that with his beautiful, pregnant wife and his adorable niece.

Once he'd helped Charlotte clean up the mystery mess—because there's no way that orange liquid-looking stuff was carrots in that jar—Anthony had told Charlotte to put on her swimsuit and cover-up. They were spending the day outdoors. Of course, that basically told her what they'd be doing, but she didn't know he'd packed a special picnic lunch for the three of them.

Choosing the adult menu had been simple, it was the culinary choice for the eight-month-old that had given him pause. He'd packed the formula, bottles with filtered water, some "veggies" and those puff-looking snacks.

Hopefully, he'd remembered everything. Running over the checklist in his mind, he drew a total blank when Charlotte came into the room with Lily on her hip.

"Is that what you're wearing?"

Her silver bikini covered only what was necessary, and a small, sheer piece of white cloth was tied around her waist.

She glanced down, then back up. "You told me to put on my suit."

The look on her face, that smirk with a gleam in her eye, told him she was not only torturing him on purpose, she was enjoying every minute of it. This was the playful side, the flirty side he'd missed. They hadn't flirted in a long time. Instead, they'd been on a cycle of fighting, fast sex and awkward silence.

But now they were getting back to how they used to be before he let his career become his mistress. Damn, it felt good to be in love again.

"We need to put sunscreen on Lily before we leave so it has time to soak in," he told her, pulling the bottle from the tote sitting by the front door.

"I'm very impressed that you thought of that."

He squirted a small amount into his hands and rubbed them over the baby's soft, pudgy arms, legs and face. "I read about it online. I may be new to this parenting gig, and I'm going to make my share of mistakes, but I've been trying to learn more and more about babies and safety. I'm getting a crash course with hands-on training."

Charlotte laughed as she rubbed a fingertip over Lily's nose to smooth in the rest of the white sunscreen.

"What's so funny?" he asked.

"Your doing all this research. I just had a visual of you online at some Mommy's Forum reading all the dos and don'ts of motherhood."

Okay, so he wouldn't tell her that's precisely how he'd picked up some of his parenting info. Those forums were helpful and, in his defense, he was doing this to be the best father he could possibly be. To both babies.

He opened the door and grabbed the bulging tote. Who knew a little one needed so much stuff for one short outing?

"Are you ready?"

She moved ahead of him and he wished he didn't know which was more appealing: Charlotte coming or going. Both views provided an eyeful that he certainly appreciated but didn't want the rest of Tahoe to enjoy, as well. This was his wife, his view and for his hands only.

He felt so much love for her. He just worried, once the baby came and if he was indeed the director of Olivia's biopic, how he would still find time to keep Charlotte happy and give her the time and attention the marriage needed.

But he'd find a way. He wanted it all and he refused to half-ass any of his roles.

"You okay?" Charlotte asked, turning to face him in the car.

He glanced her way, drinking in the site of his beautiful, loving wife. "More than okay. This is going to be a great day."

Once they got to the beach, found the perfect spot and set up a small tent to keep Lily mostly in the shade, Anthony was more than ready to test the waters.

Charlotte slid free of her silver flip-flops and her wrap, which really did nothing to hide those curves that begged for his hands to roam over them. She eased down with Lily and took out a toy shovel and pail and started scooping.

"Want to bring her into the water for a bit?" he asked.

"I will in a minute. I'm going to build a sand castle so she can knock it down."

Anthony stared at all that glorious bare skin on Charlotte and frowned. "You didn't put any sunscreen on."

Charlotte tossed him a look over her shoulder. "You're not seriously going to use that clichéd excuse to get your hands on me, are you?"

He leaned down, his body casting a shadow over her. "I don't need a lame excuse to get my hands on you, Charlie."

Lily smacked the shovel against Charlotte's arm and giggled. How that child knew when to lighten the mood was a mystery.

"I'm going to take a dip," he told her, standing and pulling his T-shirt over his head. "You should both feel free to join me after you put on your sunscreen. Can't have all that beautiful skin burned."

Maybe the temperature of the lake would cool him off, but he doubted it. He'd seen his wife naked and touched every inch of her countless times, but the sight of her in that scrap of a bikini with all her luscious curves, knowing he couldn't touch her, made him want her all the more.

He swam for a while and when Charlotte finally brought

Lily into the water, they all played and laughed at Lily's squeals and splashes. He loved seeing Charlotte love this baby as if she were her own. Even though another baby really worried him, he knew Charlotte would be wonderful, and he was anxious to see that mother-child bond with his own baby.

Once they ate lunch, which proved to be a lot less messy than breakfast, Lily was more than ready for her afternoon nap and Anthony was ready to get Charlotte back home, where she could put some damn clothes on…or take the rest off and let him inspect her tan lines.

He'd seen men do double, and triple, takes in her direction. But that was fine. How could he fault them for having excellent taste in women?

Lily fell asleep before they'd pulled out of the parking lot. Once they arrived back home, Charlotte carefully eased her from her car seat and carried her to her crib.

Anthony stood outside the master suite and waited, his control about to snap.

"I think she had fun," Charlotte whispered as she closed the baby's door. "I need to check my email for this fundraiser, then I'm going to grab a quick shower and get this sand out of my hair."

A shower was the perfect idea.

"I'm going to go ahead and hop in the shower myself." He stepped closer, running a fingertip along her pink cheek. "You're not too tired from all that are you? I want to make sure you're rested."

Her breath hitched. Good. He didn't remove his hand.

"I'm fine," she told him, looking up into his eyes. "I actually feel great. I had a wonderful time today."

For a minute, neither spoke. He stepped back, allowing his hand to fall to his side. The timeless game of predator to prey. He wanted her and he had no doubt she knew it. She'd worn those scraps on purpose and tortured him for hours.

"I'll let you get to your work," he told her, turning to go into the master suite where an oversized shower awaited him.

He had no doubt—email or no email—she'd be joining him in that shower.

Charlotte knew the dangerous game Anthony was playing. And, mercy, did she want him. She wanted to go into that shower and have him make sure every last grain of sand was rinsed from her body.

She hadn't missed the way his eyes had devoured her body at the beach…she was still tingling.

She'd seen such a change in Anthony since coming to Tahoe. The way he placed her needs before his own, the tender way he was with Lily. Everything about him screamed "family man."

Would he be happy with that? She certainly didn't want to take his career away. She didn't want him to resent her or be stuck in a life he wasn't happy with. But she did want him to know that family always came above a career. And with this baby on the way, she prayed she carried it to full term and Anthony stayed committed to their marriage and children.

Images of him laughing with Lily, of him feeding her and rocking her to sleep, flooded her mind. He loved that baby and Charlotte knew that he loved her, too. More than she ever thought someone could love her. She had no doubt he was going to try to be the man this marriage needed, the man she needed. He'd been so up-front with his emotions…behaving in a way he'd never done before. He was so attentive, so loving.

Charlotte covered her bare stomach with her hand and smiled. This child they'd created would not grow up without both parents. Charlotte knew this marriage wasn't cured or perfect, but they were most certainly on the right track and she couldn't wait to get started in the next chapter of their life as a family.

And it all started with a fresh shower to wash away the past.

Thirteen

The click of the bathroom door was music to Anthony's ears. After their turning point last night, he wanted to strengthen that intimate bond.

The open, walk-in shower left the entire bathroom visible to him without the barrier of a glass door. With textured tiles and a number of nozzles dotting the three walls, this shower had been made with just this purpose in mind—to make love to his wife with the feel of being in the open. The mirrors directly across from the shower only provided an even more erotic backdrop.

Too bad he hadn't taken advantage of this getaway home more often with her. He planned to rectify that from now on.

He turned to face the open side as Charlotte stared at him from across the room. Still clad in only her bikini and the sheer wrap around her rounded hips, she set the baby monitor on the counter and tilted her head.

"Looks like enough room for me," she said with a smile as

she reached behind her back and untied the straps of her bikini top.

With a flick of her wrist, she sent the material soaring across the room to slap against his bare, wet chest. He caught the garment and smiled.

"Plenty of room," he assured her.

She shimmied out of her wrap and bottoms and moved toward him. He didn't even try to hide how he was devouring her with his eyes, much the way he intended to do with his hands and mouth in seconds.

At the edge of the lip to the shower, Charlotte hesitated and looked into his eyes once again. "I've needed this. Us together like this."

"Me, too," he told her, extending his hand to help her over the short tiled edge. "I just was blind and couldn't see how desperately I needed you. You brought me to my knees and I'm a stronger man for it."

Her delicate hand slipped into his as she stepped up next to him, her lush body instantly wet, instantly molded to his own. He put everything else, even the pregnancy, out of his mind. For now he just wanted Charlotte. The outside world didn't exist. But the need, the desire he had for his wife, the woman who could make him turn his life around, couldn't wait.

"I've missed you," he whispered, raining kisses over her bare shoulder. "Last night was amazing, but let me show you again how much I need you."

Her hands came up to frame his face, forcing him to look her in the eyes. "I can't wait," she told him.

Too bad.

"Always in a rush." He cupped her hands with his own. "This is a new beginning for us and I'm taking my time. From now on, I'm devoting my time to you, to this family."

Her eyes darted down, her teeth worried her bottom lip. Anthony bent down, capturing those lips with his. He pulled their hands between their bodies, letting the hot water wash over them as he claimed her mouth.

"Trust me," he murmured against her lips. "Trust this. Happiness from here on out."

With a brief nod, she stood on her tiptoes to take his mouth again. Anthony let go of her hands; he had more important body parts to explore. Holding hands could be done in public. What he had in mind couldn't.

His hands roamed over her hot, wet skin as she pressed herself further against him. She was trying to kill him, but he would remain in control here and they'd both benefit in the end.

Backing her against the tile, he took her hands and held them above her head, easing back to gaze down into her eyes. Droplets ran down her face, the long column of her throat and disappeared in the valley between her breasts. He couldn't wait to lick those droplets off and make her writhe beneath him. Nothing could pull him from this moment, unless the baby began screaming through the monitor.

"Touch me, Anthony."

He smiled. "I am. For the first time in a long time, I'm going to touch every part of you. Starting with your heart."

With a gentle kiss to her lips, he made good on the promise to himself to follow those droplets running the course of her lush body. He worked his way from her jaw, down her neck and over her shoulders, all the while holding her arms above her head. She arched against him and he needed no further invitation to capture one of her pebbled nipples in his mouth.

He closed his mouth over her breast, shivering when she groaned. She begged, she cried out, but Anthony didn't move any faster as he made love to her, one luscious body part at a time.

By the time he moved to the other breast, she was panting and he was more than ready to take her.

He dropped to his knees, kissed her stomach where their

baby grew and stared up at her. "You're so beautiful, Charlie. I'll never take you for granted again."

Kissing her still-flat stomach one more time, he came to his feet and framed her face, taking her mouth once again. This time his hands roamed all on their own—one cupped her breast, the other slid down her abdomen to settle between her legs. As she grasped his shoulders, she widened her stance and tilted her hips, silently showing him what she needed, what he wanted to give.

He stroked his hand over her. Her quick breath, her arched back, the water sluicing all around them had him gritting his teeth to hold himself in check.

"Anthony...I'm..."

She shattered against him and he watched her head tilt back against the tile, eyes closed, mouth slightly open as she cried out. When her body ceased trembling, he led her to the tiled bench seat along one of the back walls of the shower. When he sat down, she came to stand between his legs.

With her hands on either side of his face, she looked down at him and smiled. "I love you, Anthony."

His heart swelled and he knew that this second chance they were taking was certainly not deserved on his part, but he was so thankful, he was going to grasp it with both hands and never let go. No matter the fear he had of this second baby, he would be strong and take charge as head of this family.

He gripped her waist and pulled her forward until she rested a leg on either side of his thighs. Once she straddled him, he smoothed her wet hair back from her face and laughed.

"What?" she asked.

"We're going to drown if we stay in here much longer."

She smiled, wrapping her arms around his neck. "I think we'll be fine."

At the same time her lips claimed his, she sank down on him. Damn that woman knew how to move. He should've known she'd take control as soon as he let his guard down.

But if getting pushed around by a woman who wanted him was punishment, he'd gladly pay the penalty.

As her hips rocked back and forth, he tore his mouth from hers to capture a breast. One thing hadn't changed in their ups and downs...he still loved her body and thoroughly enjoyed showing her.

When she picked up the rhythm, he gripped her waist and enjoyed the slide of her body beneath his hands. She grabbed hold of his shoulders and leaned her forehead against his as she shook, her eyes locked on his. And that's when he finally relinquished control.

He let the climax and the woman of his dreams take him over the edge.

Fourteen

"Be honest about this pregnancy. How do you feel?"

Searching for the right words to answer Charlotte's question, Anthony stared down at the flickering orange-and-red flames licking around the marred wood.

Charlotte had put Lily to bed while he'd gotten the fire pit all set up and pulled two cozy chaise lounge chairs close by. They'd sat in silence for several minutes and he knew she was thinking. He also knew she'd want him to open up about this baby.

"I'm anxious to see you grow with my child," he told her honestly. "But I'd be a fool not to be scared about bringing another innocent into the mix."

Silence once again settled between them. Anthony wondered if he'd said the wrong thing, but he had to be straight. He would've kept the fear to himself, but she'd asked and he wasn't about to lie.

"But you know I'm a firm believer in fate and that everything happens for a reason," he went on. "I also know that once we get back to L.A. and start talking to a marriage counselor, that should reinforce the foundation of our marriage."

Charlotte reached the narrow distance between the chairs and clasped his hand. "Well, you're willing to talk to someone—that's a big step in the right direction. You're already so wonderful with Lily. Just imagine how amazing it will be to hold your very own child."

Now he would have two children and Charlotte depending on him. Financial dependence didn't worry him at all. Yet he was just getting back what he wanted and now he was blindsided by Lily and another baby. But he wasn't lying when he said he believed everything happened for a reason. He only hoped and prayed the timing was right and that they could indeed make this work.

If Charlie ever walked away from him again, he was certain he wouldn't be able to handle it.

"I won't let you down," he told her, waiting until her eyes met his. "Never again."

For so long he'd thought all she needed was a padded bank account, a lavish house to throw parties and the backing to keep her donations to the Children's Hospital up-to-date, but she'd really only needed one thing: love. His undivided attention, unconditional love and never-ending support. She'd need that love now more than ever and so would these innocent babies.

And after all they'd been through, he deserved nothing, yet she continued to give everything…even a baby. He only prayed she would stay after the ninety days.

"I love you, Charlotte. I never told you enough, but I love you more than I can say and you give me so much more than I deserve."

"You gave me something, too." Her free hand settled over her flat belly. "But what if something happens? God, Anthony, I'm scared to death."

He pulled their joined hands up to his mouth and kissed hers. "I've already told you, this baby will be fine. You and

I are obviously fighters or we wouldn't still be together. Our baby will be strong, healthy and beautiful, just like her mother."

And in the next several months, he would work on a way to nail this director job with Bronson, gain custody of Lily permanently and cement this bridge that kept collapsing between him and Charlotte. He never again wanted to feel vulnerable or out of control. He refused to lose anything he cared about ever again.

"What are you doing?" Charlotte laughed.

Anthony peered from behind the leather sofa with a small movie camera in hand, the red light blinking.

"Filming the two of you playing on the floor," he explained as he crawled on his knees with one hand on the floor.

Charlotte picked up another oversized block and stacked it on top the others. "And this requires you to crawl?"

He grinned from behind the camera. "I wanted to get down here on your level. If I'm standing above you I don't capture the moment as well."

Charlotte rolled her eyes and looked at Lily, who was chewing and slobbering all over a red block with her big blue eyes fixed on Anthony. "Did you hear that, sweetheart? Uncle Anthony is always the director, even in his downtime."

Anthony hit a switch that caused the camera to beep, then set the device down on the floor. "Charlotte, I didn't mean for you to think—"

"Anthony." She looked over at him, seeing the sincerity on his handsome face. "I'm kidding. I'm glad you're taking home movies of Lily. I wasn't implying anything else. Okay?"

He smiled, put the camera back up into position and clicked the button again. "And here are my two favorite ladies," he said, more than likely for the camera. "Playing blocks on our last day at the lake."

Charlotte glanced toward the window and sighed. "I wish it

would clear up. I'd love to take Lily for a walk, but I'm pretty tired after yesterday."

And last night, but she wouldn't say that with the camera running. Who knew who would watch that film in later years.

"Olivia and Victoria are anxious for us to get home," Anthony told her. "They'll be at the house tomorrow to see our little Lily Bug."

Charlotte was pretty anxious herself to see Anthony's birth mother and sister in the privacy of their own home. Too often where Olivia Dane went, some sort of media entourage followed. Besides, she wanted them to get to know Lily better and share the good news of the second baby on the way.

She smiled at Anthony. "We're pretty blessed, aren't we?"

He moved the camera away from his face for just a moment, and she caught the flicker of a smile and a twinkle in his eyes. "Beyond what I deserve."

Charlotte continued building with the blocks, showing Lily how they stacked, but the eight-month-old was more interested in squealing and knocking them back down. There was no way she could be around this baby and not smile. She was too precious, too full of life. And Rachel was missing it all.

Tears filled her eyes. One escaped and slid down her cheek.

Anthony put the camera aside and moved toward her, taking a seat beside her. "Hey, what's wrong? You were just smiling."

"My mind wandered," she told him, handing Lily another block. "Every time I'm playing with her or rocking her, I think of Rachel. I feel sick knowing she'll never see this sweet baby grow up. Then I wonder how you'd get along with Lily and our baby if something happened to me."

Anthony put an arm around her, squeezing her close against his side. "Dry those tears, Charlie. We are the happiest we've been in a long time."

"You haven't talked about Rachel very much." Charlotte nestled her head against his shoulder, breathing in his masculine scent, relishing his strong, secure hold. "I worry that you keep so much bottled inside, Anthony."

He kissed the top of her head. "I think of her nearly all day. I'm sad Lily won't know how loving her mother was, but what we can do to make sure Rachel's legacy lives on is to talk about Rachel and show Lily pictures as she gets older. I definitely want Rachel to be part of this."

Charlotte's heart melted. "I couldn't agree more. Lily needs to know how much her mother wanted her, how much she was loved."

Lily tossed a wet, slobbery block that bounced right off Anthony's forehead.

"Well, at least she's got good aim," he laughed. "Maybe she'll be a softball player."

Charlotte laughed through her tears, thankful for the life she'd been given.

Fifteen

"Oh, my darling. Let me see that baby."

Charlotte stood at the base of the steps holding Lily when Olivia, the Grand Dane herself, barely had taken a step into their Hollywood Hills home. The woman was even more beautiful than the movies had made her out to be. She was stunning, classy and overly thrilled to be called "Grandma." Quite a juxtaposition.

"Come on, Lily Bug," Anthony said, taking the excited baby from Charlotte's arms and handing her over to his mother. "She's a bit squirmy today."

Olivia's face lit up as she took the baby. "Oh, I love her. She's just the sweetest little angel. Yes, you are."

Charlotte smiled and cautiously moved forward when Anthony extended his hand to her. This was what she'd missed growing up. Togetherness, the bond that comes from unconditional, familial love.

"I'm so glad you could come, Mrs. Dane."

Olivia waved a hand. "Oh, call me Olivia, darling. We're family, for heaven's sake."

Just then the door opened once more and a stunning beauty stepped in. "Sorry. I had to finish that call," Victoria said, sliding her phone into her designer handbag.

Charlotte stepped forward and smiled. "Welcome to our home. If you'd like to come into the living room, Anthony can get your bags."

"Sure thing." He closed the gap and gave Victoria a kiss on her cheek. "You can hold Lily if you can get her away from Olivia."

Victoria looked over to her mother, who was cooing with silly puckered lips. "Oh, I'll get her away," she assured. "I *have* to hold that baby."

Charlotte led them into the open living area where one entire wall was filled with floor-to-ceiling windows and glass double doors to allow any guest to enjoy the beautiful view of the lush flower gardens. Charlotte had always worked very closely with the groundskeepers and prided herself on maintaining the gardens with a tropical feeling.

She had no reason to be nervous with Olivia and Victoria staying here. Anthony had invited them to spend the weekend as a family and Charlotte thought that was a great idea. To see him embracing every aspect of his family, trying to mold the two sets together, really warmed her heart. He had taken a giant leap from living and breathing movies to becoming a family man. She wanted him to be able to do both, but she was certainly relieved that he'd opened his eyes to the fact that his career had become an obsession.

"This is just gorgeous," Victoria said, running her hand along the marble mantel. "I'm thinking of renovating my home and I've been looking at some marble chips."

Charlotte came to stand beside Victoria. "I love this shade of gray. It's dark enough to look black, but soft enough not to be so harsh."

"You are too precious. Yes, you are."

Charlotte and Victoria looked at each other and laughed at Olivia's baby talk across the room.

"My mother has wanted a baby in this family forever," Victoria added. "Between Lily and Bella, Bronson and Mia's baby, the heat is off me for a while."

Charlotte forced herself not to touch her stomach. They didn't know about the pregnancy yet, and since this was Anthony's family, she'd let him decide when to make the happy announcement.

"Do you want children?" Charlotte asked, then realized she'd always hated when people asked her that. "Sorry, that's not really my business."

Victoria reached over, patting her arm. "No need to apologize. I'd love to fill my house with babies. I just have some career goals I'd like to accomplish first."

Charlotte glanced over to Lily, Olivia and Anthony. "We've only been her guardian for a few weeks, but she's certainly changed our lives. I love her so much."

"This little sweetie would be impossible not to love."

Olivia held Lily up in the air, puckered her lips and made even more silly noises.

Victoria laughed and leaned over to Charlotte. "If you want to do anything at all, like take a few hours and read a book or go shopping, do it while my mother is here. She will do everything for this baby. You and Anthony could leave the house and she wouldn't even notice."

Watching Olivia with Lily gave her a sense of belonging. Lily wasn't related to Olivia in any way, shape or form, but the woman had instantly taken to her as if she was her very own.

This bond the Dane family had wasn't just a show for the media and the paparazzi. They were genuine and caring and perfect for her and Anthony at this stage in their lives. Perfect for the baby she carried and for Lily.

"Would you two like anything to drink or eat?" Charlotte

asked, feeling that she should at least offer something to her guests. "I made some banana muffins earlier and I was thinking of grilling fish for dinner."

Olivia threw her a glance and smiled. "Darling, sit down. We don't need to be waited on."

"Nothing for me, thanks." Victoria moved to sit on the sofa, obviously trying to get to Lily. "I snacked the whole way here and I need to stop that. I get the munchies when I'm creating a new design."

Feeling more relaxed with Anthony's new family, Charlotte sat next to Victoria on the sofa. "What are you working on? Can I ask?"

"Oh, I don't mind talking shop," Victoria told her, crossing her long legs and easing back onto the cushions. "I'm in the middle of drawing up a few wedding gown designs for my friend Stefan. He's the prince of Galini Isle, a small island country off the coast of Greece, and since this will be for the princess and soon-to-be queen and I've never designed wedding dresses, I'm a little nervous. I've never met his fiancée, so that's why I'm working on several choices for her."

Olivia, still bouncing a happy, giggly Lily, said, "Oh, you have no reason to worry. They wanted the best and they've got her. Your gowns are unique and exquisite. Besides, you and Stefan go way back, honey. He wouldn't have asked if he had any doubts."

Victoria sighed. "I hope the bride is happy with Stefan choosing the designer, Mom."

Charlotte couldn't imagine designing for royalty. She couldn't even imagine knowing royalty. Talk about glamorous.

"I'm sure other designers will have copies of your gown within days after the ceremony," Olivia added. "You'll be busier than you already are. One of these days you're going to have to slow down."

Anthony sat up straighter on the arm of the sofa and

laughed. "Slow down? Is that Olivia Dane giving advice on slowing down?"

"Exactly," Victoria chimed in. "She'll never work at anything other than warp speed."

Anthony glanced across the room and winked. Charlotte nearly melted. He looked so happy, so bright with his family here.

He'd asked her to give him ninety days until the hearing for Lily's permanent guardianship, but Charlotte knew after their weeks away in Tahoe they would last much, much longer than three months.

And she couldn't wait until the hearing so Lily was legally and permanently theirs.

"Would you like to tell them our news?" Anthony asked during a lull in the conversation, still smiling across the room.

Charlotte swallowed as both women turned to look at her. "Why don't you?"

"We're expecting," he said proudly. "Should be a spring baby."

Olivia squealed with delight, causing Lily to squeal as well and clap her hands. "Oh, I wanted grandbabies so badly and here I'm going to have three within one year. I am a blessed woman."

Victoria leaned over and hugged Charlotte. "That's wonderful. How are you feeling?"

Charlotte couldn't get over the way these women were talking with her as if they'd known her forever and they were very eager to hear about her life. Did they know about the separation she and Anthony had had for several months? If they did, they were being very discreet and noble about it. Thank God, because she really wanted to move forward and celebrate their marriage and babies.

"I'm okay. I get a little queasy in the evenings, but nothing in the mornings, as the books say."

"I remember when I was pregnant with Anthony," Olivia

said, settling back into the chair and turning Lily to face out-ward on her knee. "I never felt better. I thought pregnant women were just complaining to get attention. I found out differently when I got pregnant with Bronson and Victoria. I was sick the entire time with both pregnancies."

Charlotte inwardly groaned at the thought of being sick and nauseous for months.

"I can't wait to have another baby to spoil," Olivia went on.

Victoria laughed. "You've already spoiled Bella and she's only a couple months old. Her room looks like FAO Schwarz set up shop."

Charlotte laughed and glanced at Anthony, who just smiled. Something passed between them. Something private and... wonderful. His smile widened as his gaze dropped to her belly and back up to her eyes. He mouthed "Love you" and Char-lotte's smile widened as she tapped her heart.

She was so glad Anthony's family was here. Victoria and Olivia may be stunning women who hailed from the land of perfection, also known as Hollywood, but these women were down-to-earth and seemed very genuine.

Settling a hand over her stomach, Charlotte was thankful her baby would have such amazing women in its life.

"Well, I hate to steal your thunder, but I have some news of my own," Victoria announced.

Charlotte laughed. "You're not stealing our thunder at all. We'd love more good news."

Reaching into the pocket of her slimming black capris, Vic-toria pulled out a ring and slid it on. "Alex and I got engaged two days ago."

Charlotte stared at the glittering diamond. "Oh, that's so wonderful. I'm so happy for you."

Anthony glanced to his mother. "Since you're not squeal-ing, I assume you knew?"

Olivia took her eyes off Lily and tilted her head. "Anthony, really. I'm her mother. I was the first person she called."

"Congrats, Victoria." Anthony moved over to give her a hug. "Is this Alex Stone? The actor, right?"

Victoria beamed. "Yes. He's only been in a few movies, but he's really amazing."

Charlotte couldn't believe how much love and happiness surrounded her—she felt blessed. Anthony had such a secure family, and Charlotte had no doubt this newly formed connection would last a lifetime. She was extremely fortunate to be included in that bond.

Most people didn't get second chances, but she and Anthony had found their way back. With the help of talking to a counselor and Anthony reprioritizing his life, they were going to make it. She had no doubt.

"Insomnia was always my friend when my life was less than stable."

Charlotte glanced up from her laptop, which she'd set up in the breakfast area off the kitchen. Clad in black silk pajamas with matching slippers, Olivia removed a bottle of water from the refrigerator and moved over to the table.

"May I have a seat, dear?" Olivia asked, her perfectly manicured hand resting on the back of the wooden chair.

Charlotte had a feeling not many people told the Grand Dane of Hollywood no, so she gestured for her to sit. "Of course."

"You're too kind to tell me I'm interrupting your work." With a smile, Olivia took a seat and uncapped her water. "I hear you're the woman behind all the wonderful things at the Children's Hospital."

Not wanting to take all the credit, Charlotte simply smiled. "I don't know if I'm the only woman behind it, but I do work with a great group to make sure our children have the best medical care, no matter what their financial circumstances."

Olivia took a sip—a woman like that didn't gulp. "Children are obviously an important part of your life."

Because cramps had woken her up and just the thought of

something happening to the baby had her scared, she'd come downstairs to call the doctor's office and leave a message. When he'd called her back, he'd assured her that cramps were normal, but she should probably take it easy just to be sure and to call if the pain increased or if there was any bleeding.

Exiting the program she wasn't even focused on before the interruption, Charlotte nodded and closed the computer. "They are. I've met some amazing kids through my work at the hospital and I'm eager to see this new wing that's opening."

"You have an amazing kid yourself, too."

Charlotte smiled. "Lily *is* wonderful."

Olivia reached across and laid her hand over Charlotte's. "It's okay to be nervous. I know you and Anthony have had some issues and now you have this baby to care for, Rachel's death to mourn and a baby on the way. Is there anything I can do?"

Charlotte shouldn't be surprised that Olivia knew about their marital problems, but she was surprised at how well the woman managed to figure out emotions that Charlotte wasn't even sure she was feeling.

"I won't lie and say it hasn't been a difficult few years for us," Charlotte told her. "But we are working on this marriage, and the trip to Tahoe really helped steer us back in the right direction. He was shocked over the pregnancy, but I think he's excited, too."

A slight laugh escaped her as she looked down to her closed laptop. "I'm sorry, this is just all a little surreal for me."

Olivia pulled her hand back, clasped her water bottle and tilted her head. "What's that, my dear?"

"I'm sitting here with one of the most iconic women in movies, wearing pajamas at midnight and pouring my heart out as if we're at some adult slumber party."

Olivia laughed. "I never had a slumber party as a child, so I'm honored to have my first one with my beautiful daughter-in-law."

Charlotte's throat clogged with tears. "You think of me as your daughter-in-law?"

"Well, of course." With a warm smile, Olivia eased forward in her chair. "I may have just come back into Anthony's life, but we've embraced this mother-son relationship and I consider you just as much my family as Mia."

Charlotte let out a watery laugh. "You don't know how much that means to me, Olivia. I'm not sure if you know my family background…"

"I know enough to know you need family just as much as Anthony right now." Olivia reached for Charlotte's hands. "I know you grew up with less than comfortable means, and I know you had a sister who passed of leukemia. I think that combination is what has made you the strong, humble woman you are today. The work you've done with the Children's Hospital is beyond remarkable. You have seriously risen above your past and made something of yourself and, by doing so, you've blessed so many lives."

Charlotte sank back in her seat, unsure how to react to the facts Olivia knew and the compliments she so easily doled out.

"I'm surprised Anthony told you all that," Charlotte said, more thinking aloud than asking Olivia for an answer.

Olivia patted her hand. "Actually, when he told me he was praising you. He was upset over the separation and was telling me how he was going to fight for you because he needed you and he felt you needed him and a family. I apologize if my knowing makes you uncomfortable."

"Not at all," Charlotte told her. "I just didn't know he'd opened up to you about our marriage. He used to be so closed off, so private."

"Yes," Olivia agreed. "But you are good for him, Charlotte. More than you know. You two are going to make a wonderful family, no matter what your past—or his."

"I hope so, but it was my background that nearly ruined our marriage," Charlotte confessed. "Anthony wants to give me all that I never had. Beautiful houses, nice cars, trips around the world. But it took him a while to see that I just needed—"

"His love," Olivia finished.

Charlotte nodded. "Yeah. He's certainly spoiled me with everything I could ever ask for, but for years I seriously felt as if I was getting shoved aside for another project, each one bigger than the last."

"His heart was in the right place. His head obviously was not, but he did want to give you a secure life."

Charlotte knew this, knew Anthony loved her and had never strayed from their vows. She knew his heart had always been with her. Unfortunately, it had taken quite a turn of life-altering events to get him to realize his priorities were in the wrong order and needed to be reshuffled.

"That secure life and knowing how much we love each other is what is helping us get our marriage back on track."

Olivia smiled. "I was married to the love of my life for over thirty years before he passed. There's nothing better than spending your life with the one person who makes you complete, who knows you better than anybody and who would change his life to make yours perfect."

Olivia came to her feet, kissed the top of Charlotte's head. "Anthony may not be the best when it comes to juggling work and family, but I know he loves you and I've seen how committed he is to his family. I'll say it again. You're one blessed woman, Charlotte."

Once Charlotte was alone again, she folded her hands together and rested her head against them. Love swelled inside her for the family she had now with Anthony's birth mother and sister.

Yes, she was a blessed woman. And in a few weeks, when Lily was permanently theirs, they could move forward with their life and concentrate on the upcoming birth of their own child.

Charlotte prayed for that day to come as she rubbed the cramp away low in her belly.

Sixteen

Anthony had just hung up the phone when his mother entered his office.

"Hey, come on in." He came to his feet and moved around the oversized mahogany desk, easing a hip onto the edge. "I was just coming to see where everyone was."

Olivia took a seat in the leather club chair opposite his desk. "Charlotte is busy getting Lily down for a nap, Victoria is on the phone with Mia and I wanted to talk to you."

Anthony grinned. "Well, since I'm too old for the birds and the bees talk, what do you have to discuss that you sound so serious?"

Olivia smiled, crossing her legs. "Nothing near as fearful for a mother as the sex talk. This subject is much more approachable. Bronson and I have been talking, and he's asked me to discuss something with you so he can concentrate on Mia and the baby. He's a little busy right now."

To say the least. That's what had Anthony's stomach in knots, too. The great Bronson Dane was busy juggling his work and one child. How would Anthony do with two babies while repairing a marriage?

One day at a time, he told himself. He just had to concentrate on keeping his family together one day at a time so they could turn that one day into a lifetime.

Anthony focused back on Olivia. He knew what she was going to say. She was going to bring up the film that he'd been champing at the bit to direct. The film depicting the life of Olivia Dane through the decades of her remarkable career.

"I'm sure you know that Bronson is producing my biographical film. We've only recently finalized the draft of the script and the budget, and we'd love you to consider directing it."

As if any director would turn down an opportunity like this, let alone the son of the woman the movie was about. He'd been waiting for this moment, been dreaming of it. Since finding out Olivia was his mother and since Bronson had decided to do a film, he'd been aching to be part of it.

He truly had it all now.

Anthony reached out, taking Olivia's hands. "It would be an honor to work with my family on this film."

Her smile stretched across her face. "It really will be a family affair. Victoria is planning on doing the wardrobe designs, though she's never done that for a film before."

Anthony could barely contain his excitement, his relief to know that they trusted him to work on such an important film. Granted, he was one of the top directors in Hollywood, but it hadn't been that long ago that he and Bronson couldn't even be in the same room. Now they were half brothers and getting ready to work on a film together.

How would Charlotte react? Would she be excited for him? Would she want to come on set with him to see how things are done? He'd always wanted her to, but she had never seen him at work.

Maybe this time she would. Maybe with these new steps

in making their marriage a joint effort, she'd accompany him, especially since the film was so close to his heart.

"I know you'll want to discuss this with Charlotte," Olivia went on. "You can let me know for sure later. Besides, Victoria and I really do need to get on the road. We both have so much work to do, but I hate leaving Lily."

Anthony laughed, tugging on Olivia's hands to pull her to her feet. "I've already been replaced, huh?"

She settled one perfectly manicured hand on his cheek. "Never. You're my first child—you could never be replaced."

Looking down into his mother's eyes, he couldn't help but wonder how hard it must've been for her to give him up. He couldn't imagine giving up the baby he and Charlotte had created, or Lily.

"I'm really lucky to have you in my life now," he told her, kissing her on the cheek. "I'll talk to Charlie, but I know she'll be happy with this decision."

Olivia squeezed his hand. "Just make sure she's part of your decision making, darling. Marriage is a two-way street."

That was something he should've realized long ago, but a basic fact he was learning the hard way.

"I promise to spend this evening talking with her about it and I will call you tomorrow."

"I may be at Bron and Mia's house," she told him as she turned to leave the office. "I promised them I'd babysit while they went out for the day. Why don't you take a little more time to make sure this is something you can handle right now with everything else you have going on."

His answer would still be the same if he thought about it for months.

"I don't intend to take on more than I should, especially now that I have another chance with Charlotte and a new family." He followed her out into the marble foyer. "Why don't you call me tomorrow when you're done with babysitting? We can discuss further details and my decision."

Olivia nodded. "Perfect."

* * *

Charlotte had just slid between the crisp, cool sheets when Anthony emerged from the adjoining bathroom. Wearing only black boxer briefs, he never ceased to make her heart beat faster and her body react to his sexy appeal.

Especially now that her hormones were ramped up about 200 percent and they were really working on this marriage and actually talking and opening up. Nothing was more erotic than a man baring his soul.

She pulled the edge of the sheet back on his side, inviting him to join her. She'd put on her favorite navy blue silk chemise, and even though it had pulled just a bit around her belly, she didn't think he'd even notice. She had actually smiled when she'd slid the unforgiving fabric on. This was the first thing that was a bit snug around her midsection.

She prayed her belly continued to grow, though, because the alternative was inconceivable. She'd been cramping slightly every day, but the pain hadn't grown any worse. Still, that fear had lodged deep within her.

"Do you think we could take another trip before this baby comes?" she asked as he settled in beside her.

The coarse hair on his thigh rubbed her bare one. The simple contact had her remembering the short few months when she was sleeping alone, missing his warmth beside her, longing for just one more intimate touch.

"Absolutely," he told her, picking up her hand, kissing it and laying it on his lap. "When and where?"

"Anywhere is fine. I was thinking after the court date we could have a nice extended vacation to celebrate."

"I may be back to work then, but we'll figure something out."

A whisper of fear slid through her. Was he already going to push them aside in an attempt to keep this movie? Would he really postpone their family time so he could spend his days worrying over the set, the script and the actors?

She couldn't think negatively. If she wanted to keep this marriage strong, she had to think positively. But in the back of her mind, she couldn't help but worry how this would all play out once he started working again.

Anthony tugged her closer to settle in the crook of his arm. "What do you have going on under here?"

His touch sidetracked her thoughts. "Enjoy it now. This is probably the last time this will be on me for a while. It's a little tight around my waist."

His hand cupped her satin-covered belly. "You'll always look amazing, and now that you're carrying my child you're even more beautiful." He sounded so eager, excited for another baby.

"I'm so scared, Anthony. I've been cramping and I just can't lose this child."

His gaze jerked back up to hers. "Did you call the doctor? Why haven't you told me?"

"I didn't want you to worry," she confessed. "The doctor said my uterus is stretching and that's normal, but I just know last time—"

"No." He put a finger over her lips. "This isn't last time."

The tenderness she saw in his eyes, felt in his touch in recent weeks, gave her new hope.

She grabbed his hands, lacing her fingers through his. "I know. And the doctor said to take it easy and not lift a lot. He's confident I'll be fine."

"Then we won't borrow trouble," he told her, kissing her slightly on the lips. "We're moving forward, Charlie, and this baby inside you is part of our future."

Oh, she hoped so. There was so much she wanted from her life. She wanted her marriage to work more than anything. Wanted her children to have a stable home life, unlike the one she came from. And, selfishly, she wanted her marriage to last forever. She wanted that love she'd seen so many times in the movies her husband directed.

Too bad he'd had difficulties directing his own marriage.

But now he seemed devoted, changed and the family man she needed him to be. Of course, he was also getting ready to start the biggest project of his life. Only time would tell how he reacted and worked everything out.

"Sorry I interrupted you with my scare. I don't want you to think I'm selfish," she told him, toying with the beading on the comforter. "I don't want you to feel that this family is taking you from your job or that you're sacrificing anything."

"I don't feel that way at all, Charlie." He took her hand in his and squeezed. "I want to go to the new-wing dedication next week, if that's okay. Olivia could watch Lily for us."

Charlotte couldn't suppress the grin, the swift intake of breath that held so much hope. "Really? You've always been so busy in the past."

"I'll never be too busy for you or our children. Never. I didn't realize how important this was to you before. I'm sorry, Charlotte. You're worth everything to me." He tipped her chin and looked into her eyes. "Every bit of fear I had when you walked out that door, every second I didn't have you with me, made me realize that even if you did decide on the divorce, I had to try. I had to give every bit of my heart to you and take the chance. I can't give up the memories we still have to make."

There were no words. Nothing could make this moment any more perfect. Here was the man she'd needed, wanted, loved. Here was the man she'd married, knowing he would be everything she'd ever wanted—strong yet gentle, powerful yet vulnerable.

"I love you, Charlotte."

She turned to face him fully. "I know you do. I see it when you look at me, talk to me. Make love to me."

Leaning toward her, he captured her lips in a soft, loving way that shot hope and joy straight to her heart.

He eased back, cupping her cheek in one strong hand. "Since

we're starting new here, I do have something to discuss with you."

"What is it?"

"Olivia approached me earlier with the job I've been waiting on."

Charlotte smiled. "To direct the movie depicting her life?"

"You know I've wanted to do this since the whole discovery of her being my mother and finding out they were going to make this film, but I won't if you think we're not at a good point in our marriage to handle this."

And what kind of selfish woman would deny her husband the project of a lifetime, especially when that project involved his birth mother and brother?

Added to that, this was the first time he'd asked her opinion before signing on to a movie. In the past he'd simply made the decision himself and told her his upcoming schedule.

"Anthony, I wouldn't expect you to give up this dream." She settled a hand on his bare chest. "I can't tell you how happy I am that you discussed this with me first. You know you've never mentioned movies or projects before you start working on them. You've never made it part of our lives. Always before it was Anthony the husband or Anthony the director. It's nice having both sides of you in bed with me."

He reached for her once again, pressing her back against the pillows as he came to lie over her. "Is that so? Well, which side of me do you want to see now?"

She curled her arms around his neck. "All of them."

Seventeen

"I can't get over how tiny she is."

Anthony stood in the corner of Bronson and Mia's living room as all the women—Charlotte, Victoria and Olivia—hovered around the sofa, oohing and aahing over Bella.

"And look at all this black hair," Charlotte went on. "Lily seems so big compared to Bella."

Mia laughed. "Well, Lily is, what…nine months old now? Bella is only two."

Anthony glanced at Bronson. At one time the two men could barely stand being on the same movie set and now, only months after discovering they were brothers, here they were sharing baby stories.

"If she weren't already pregnant, I'm sure this would convince her we needed one of our own," Anthony murmured to Bronson, trying to break the ice of the awkward silence on their side of the room.

His brother laughed. "Babies are amazing creatures. She's

been here for two months and my life is so different. I'd do anything for her."

Anthony met Charlotte's gaze, a beautiful smile beaming from her. "I know what you mean."

Bronson turned to Anthony. "Since the women are occupied, I'd like to discuss a project with you."

"Olivia's biography?" Now, this would certainly keep a conversation going and hopefully not be strained. "She spoke with me a couple days ago when she was at the house. If you're still in need of a director, I'd be honored to team up with you."

Bronson nodded. "That's a relief. Mom was really adamant about having you and I wanted the best."

Anthony laughed. "That hurt you to say, didn't it?"

"Maybe just a little." Bronson laughed. "But the film just needs that touch that only you can bring to it."

Humbled by the honest words, Anthony shrugged. "I love my work just as you do. It comes through on the screen."

"Let's have a seat." Bronson motioned to the sofa off to the side. "I don't think they'll mind if we talk shop for a few minutes."

"Not for very long, boys," Olivia scolded without turning her eyes from the baby. "We're here to see Bella and enjoy family time."

Anthony shook his head and took a seat next to Bronson. "How soon are you looking to start shooting?"

"I'd like to meet with the actors in the next month or so."

Anthony jerked back. "Do they already have the script? Seems fast."

"Their agents received it last week, but they'd all committed before reading it," Bronson confirmed. "I think they all knew this was going to be a big project. And I'm pulling out all the stops with the budget, the locations. No limits on this one. This has to be the best project either of us have ever committed to."

Anthony nodded. "I couldn't agree more. Who is reading the scripts?"

Bronson rattled off an impressive roster of A-list actors who would certainly rake in fans of all ages. Images of scenes from various points in Olivia's personal and public life filtered through his head. This would no doubt be the most important project of his career and he intended to devote his full attention to it.

With Charlotte by his side.

"Okay, that's enough," Mia said from the sofa. "No more talk of movies. You can do that later."

"I'll call you with the meeting details once I nail down all the agents and times," Bronson muttered. "We'd better go over there before the women get angry. That's never pretty."

Anthony came to his feet and joined Charlotte, who had passed a sleeping Bella off to Victoria.

"Do you want a little brother or sister?" Olivia asked Lily as she bounced her on her hip. "You're going to be the best big sister and cousin. Yes, you are."

Bronson rolled his eyes. "I hope you all don't expect me to use that silly voice when talking to the kids."

Anthony laughed. "Want me to tell you about a couple weeks ago when I pranced through the house in Tahoe wearing only my boxers and singing 'The Wheels on the Bus,' 'You Are My Sunshine' and 'The Itsy Bitsy Spider' to Lily so she'd stop crying? Charlotte was trying to draw some of the scenery with her new charcoals and Lily really wasn't my biggest fan at first. I tried it all. Believe me, you'll do that silly voice and so much more."

Victoria tapped the tip of her finger on Bella's tiny nose. "You are so precious. If your daddy isn't nice, you come find me or Uncle Anthony. We'll make him play nice."

Bronson sat on the edge of the couch. "I can see I'm going to be outnumbered."

Charlotte smiled, wrapping an arm around Anthony's waist. "Only until you give in and come to the baby side."

"I imagine these two little girls," Anthony said, looking

from Lily to Bella, "will team up and have us all wrapped around their manicured fingers in no time."

"Oh, manicures," Olivia gushed. "I can't wait until these girls get older and I can introduce them to the spa. What fun times."

Anthony patted her arm. "Let's slow down and let them be babies first. Don't go scheduling any chemical peels just yet."

Olivia sent him a smirk and Anthony knew he'd have to keep a close eye on his children so they weren't overly spoiled. At the same time, he also wanted Olivia to enjoy her grandchildren.

"At least wait until they're teenagers," he begged.

"We'll see."

"Feel free to spoil me and Mia with manicures and chemical peels," Charlotte piped up with a laugh. "Right, Mia?"

"Oh, yeah," Mia agreed. "I could so use some spa time after the last two months of little sleep."

Olivia slid her phone from her designer handbag. "I'll make appointments for us for next week."

Anthony shook his head as Olivia slipped out the door. This family was a gift, a second chance. He had no doubt that, as the family grew, there would never be a dull moment.

And Charlotte laughed and talked with his family as if she'd been with them for years. That thrilled him. This was the love and life Charlotte needed to keep that brightness in her beautiful eyes. He was just glad he realized it before it was too late.

Anthony stared at the image on the glossy photo…or rather the series of photos that the ultrasound tech had given them earlier.

"Can you believe it? Another girl." Charlotte beamed as she held the pictures in her hand. "I can't wait to tell everyone."

"I'm surprised you hadn't called them all already," he told her, kissing the top of her head.

She leaned back against his chest as he wrapped his arms around her, settling his hands on her baby bump.

"I didn't want to say it over the phone. Let's have everyone over for a family dinner."

"Really?"

She turned in his arms. "Is that okay? I mean, I just assumed it would be."

He pulled her into his arms, hugging her tight. "I think that's an excellent idea. I love that you want to get to know my new family. It's still hard to believe that Rachel's gone, and sometimes I feel as if I'm just moving on and replacing her, but…"

Charlotte eased back, cupping his cheek with her hand. "You're not replacing her at all. She would have wanted you to move on. She would want you to create this family environment for Lily. And I know it's hard, believe me—I have my moments, too—but we have to be strong. Rachel would be so proud of you."

Anthony nodded. "I know, but that doesn't make the guilt any easier to bear."

"Lily is lucky to have us, to have this bond we've made for her. That's what would've mattered to Rachel."

The question that had been heavy on his mind for several weeks pushed its way to the surface. He knew they were making headway in their marriage, but they hadn't necessarily discussed plans for once the guardianship was permanent. He assumed, but…

"What are your plans after the court hearing in a few weeks?"

Anthony watched as Charlotte blinked, opened her mouth then closed it. Silence enveloped them as he waited for her to answer.

"What?"

He smoothed a wayward strand of hair back from her cheek, tucking it behind her ear. "How can I convince you to stay after the ninety days are over?"

"I hadn't planned on leaving after the court date," she told him, turning her face into his palm. "Are you having second thoughts? With this movie coming up, are you worried about us? You've been quiet about the pregnancy. Does another baby scare you?"

"I'll be honest that the thought of caring for two babies while working and trying to keep our marriage strong is a little overwhelming." He stroked her cheek. "But I'm not giving up. I'm here for you no matter what. I'm here for these babies, too."

She closed her eyes and sighed. "I'm scared, Anthony. So scared that you'll get overwhelmed with this new project and we'll all be pushed to the side. I know you won't mean to, but the worry is still there."

He'd done this to their marriage. Over the years, he'd placed the doubts in her head, the insecurity. He had a lot of work to do to rebuild her confidence in him.

Anthony cupped both sides of her face, forcing her to look him directly in the eyes. "I know what's important and it's you, Charlotte. Babies or no babies, I wouldn't have let you get too far from me. I would've come knocking on your door once you'd had enough time to think. And I know those months I left you alone amounted to a long time—believe me, I know. I wanted to get everything wrapped up so I could come to you, then Rachel passed and I went to get Lily. My life just snowballed and fate landed me at your door anyway."

She started to speak, but he placed a finger over her lips.

"You have all my love," he went on. "I know it's not nearly enough, but you have every bit I have in me. Let's get through this court date and then we can move forward."

Tears settled into her beautiful green eyes. As one slid down her porcelain cheek, he swiped it away with the pad of his thumb.

"No more tears—happy or sad. We have a lifetime of happiness ahead of us if you'll just let me give it to you."

She glanced down to the photos of their baby growing safely inside her. "I don't know what I did to deserve you. I really thought you could never love me as much as your job. I mean, once you started getting more and more popular I was so afraid you'd still see me as the girl from the wrong side of the tracks that you started dating. That I wouldn't keep up with all the glitz and glamour. My confidence was a little low."

"No," he retorted. "You weren't confident at all. Not in yourself and not in us. But that's going to change. Where you came from is one of the reasons I fell in love with you. You never wanted this lifestyle for the fame and the material things, even though I love to shower you with every luxury. You are always eager to help others and you love with everything in you. How could I ever turn that away?"

Charlotte smiled. "You've been blindsided with two babies and now you're going to start therapy with me. I'd say you're stuck with me."

He hugged her close. "I wouldn't want to be stuck anywhere else."

Anthony wanted to embrace this new level he and Charlotte had reached in their marriage. He wanted to treasure every moment, every memory.

Damn the fear and the doubts he had about being a good father and a good husband. With Charlotte at his side he could, and would, have it all.

Eighteen

Anthony watched his wife—his beautiful, charming, powerful wife—work the room like a pro. Why hadn't he given any thought to how valuable she was years ago? Oh, he'd known she was valuable as his wife, but that's where her personal title ended.

As he stood off to the side in the Children's Hospital's open lobby, he remembered how she'd wowed the crowd when she'd spoken during the new-wing dedication ceremony. She'd brought to life her childhood heartache of losing a sister to leukemia, her past of financial woes, and she'd managed to captivate the room with her charm, her compassion and her beauty. He'd not only watched her deliver a stellar speech, he'd glanced around the room at the smiles on people's faces, the lives she'd touched, and his heart had swelled with pride.

And she was all his. She wasn't leaving, she wasn't going to move on in her life without him. She was 100 percent his and she was pregnant and glowing with their child. Her belly had started getting a little round, and the visible reminder of their love was helping calm his fears and doubts…not completely, but little by little he was becoming more used to becoming the father of another baby.

Two months ago they were just dealing with Lily and working together for her. Now they were a family. The therapy sessions had started and, much to his surprise, weren't excruciating.

How the hell had he gotten so lucky to be given another opportunity? Not only with Charlotte, but also with another family. The Danes had fully embraced him, though Bronson was understandably slower to come around, and now he had two children to add to the space in his heart where voids had once settled.

There would always be those three spots where his adoptive parents and Rachel resided, but at least he had much more love than heartache. He had so much to be thankful for, to work toward making his life mean something other than the next big blockbuster.

"Mr. Price."

Anthony turned to an elderly woman who reminded him of his mother, from the flawless complexion no doubt courtesy of one of L.A.'s finest plastic surgeons, to the regal way she held her head and shoulders.

"Yes, ma'am?" he asked.

"It is a pleasure to finally meet you in person," she gushed, laying a jeweled hand over his arm. "My name is Susan McCoy. I'm the CEO here at the Children's Hospital. I can't tell you how honored we are to have your wife on our board."

"You're a lucky woman to have someone as dedicated as Charlotte." He beamed with pride. "She's very devoted."

"She's done so much for this hospital over the years. She's put in countless hours behind the scenes and never wants any credit for her hard work." Susan sighed, just enough for the drama to really sink in. "I don't think I need to tell you how humble and giving our Charlotte is."

Anthony sipped his scotch. He knew exactly how humble and giving—make that *for*giving—his wife was.

"The way she hosts parties for the staff in your lovely home," she went on. "It's always such a shame you're away on business when she has them. I know many of the staff here would love to thank you as well for allowing us to steal so much of your wife's time."

His wife's time. The time when he'd been gone and she'd filled the void. At least something positive had come from his absence over the years. Unfortunately, she'd probably made excuse after excuse as to why he was never in attendance and she'd more than likely done so with a beautiful smile on her face, all while her heart had been breaking.

"Yes, that's her," he added because standing silent only made him look like an idiot. "She's always so giving with her time and money."

"Oh, and a few months ago when she sent one of our terminal patients to Disney with her family—that was so amazing. Make-A-Wish hadn't been able to get her, and Charlotte stepped right up to make that little girl's dream come true."

Anthony watched as Charlotte turned, looking around the room and zeroing in on him. She threw him a smile that warmed him, but he couldn't help wondering just how much his wife had done in her life while he'd been off living his. If she'd tried to tell him, had he listened? God, what a selfish prick he'd been.

Their trip to Tahoe had proven to him just how much he'd missed her, how much he needed her. But this moment, tonight, proved to him just how much he admired her, respected her.

"You two are lucky to have each other," Susan went on. "My Eddie passed three years ago this December. I always tell young couples in love to cherish every moment. You just never know when the moment will pass. Oh, and congratulations on the babies!"

Anthony turned back to Susan and smiled. "Thank you."

"Charlotte has talked about how sweet Lily is. I can't wait to see her. And with Charlotte's glowing pregnancy and her love of children, she's going to be an amazing mother."

He glanced across the room once again as Charlotte smiled, talking to a doctor.

"Yes, she is," he agreed. "I'm one lucky man."

Susan patted his arm again. "Well, I need to go see some other people, but I wanted to introduce myself and just let you know how much we appreciate everything you and your wife have done for our children."

"My pleasure," he told her with a smile.

As the CEO wove her way through the round tables, he wanted to know more. He wanted to know just how big an impact his wife had had here, but he had a feeling he already knew.

She'd thrown herself into her work, just as she did with everything else in life. Her whole heart had led her here and she continued to put others' needs ahead of her own.

Drawn to that love she so freely gave, he made his way across the open lobby, stopping to say hi to several people along the way. By the time he got to his wife, she was chatting with a group of ladies, and the soothing tone of her laughter warmed him like nothing else could.

Setting his empty glass on the high tabletop, he eased his hand on her bare back and thanked the wardrobe god who'd persuaded Charlotte to wear the strapless, knee-length, white chiffon dress. She'd said it was the only dress that was dressy, comfortable and with an empire waist to accommodate her swollen waistline. Whatever the reasons, Anthony was grateful because there wouldn't be much to unwrap her from once they returned home.

"Evening, ladies." The slight tremble from Charlotte beneath his hand had him even more anxious to get her home. "Mind if I steal my lovely wife for a moment?"

A chorus of *of course* went around, but Anthony was already steering Charlotte away from the group and toward the dimly lit hallway. He had no idea where it led, but he did know that no one was occupying it and that's all that mattered.

"Anthony," she protested. "We're being rude."

He pulled her into a doorway, away from the lights, away from the crowd, and backed her against the wall, capturing her lips.

Immediately her arms circled around his neck, her small clutch hitting his back as she opened her mouth, taking him in.

Anthony slid his hands over her waist, loving the feel of her body, now all lush and curvier. She drove him insane with want and he wondered how much longer they had to remain at the ceremony now that the dinner and speeches were over.

Charlotte moved one hand to his chest and pushed just enough to have him lifting his mouth from hers.

"Something turn you on in there?" she asked with a grin on her swollen, moist lips.

He kissed the tip of her nose. "Yeah, my amazingly sexy, caring, compassionate wife who just so happens to be glowing with the pregnancy of our child."

"I'm sweating, that's the glow." She laughed. "Seriously, what happened? You'd been mingling since my speech, then you talk to Susan and now you're devouring me…not that I'm complaining."

He caged her in with his arms on either side of her face. "I realized how giving you are to other people. I knew you were perfect for me, but when I hear so much praise from others, I'm just so proud that you're mine."

Charlotte's eyes darted down, then back up. "There's nothing to be proud of, Anthony. I love what I do. I love these kids, and anything I can do to make them happier is more than enough for me."

Anthony gently kissed her lips. "That's why you're so amazing."

"I couldn't sit by and do nothing," she told him. "Not when

there are so many children in need who either have poor health insurance or none at all. They all deserve to have healthy lives."

Anthony smiled. "The people you've touched—the children here, the staff, Lily. Me." He slid his hands up her bare arms and cupped her shoulders. "You've put a light into all our lives, and I don't think you realize how brightly you shine."

Charlotte cupped his cheek, stroking his jaw with her thumb. "I've never heard such pretty words from you. You always keep your emotions so bottled up inside."

"I didn't mean to choose to let it all out here," he confessed. "I just couldn't contain my love for you, the pride I have and how anxious I am to get to know even more of you in our next fifty years together."

Charlotte's eyes welled with unshed tears. "How long can you keep going with the charm?"

"For the rest of your life," he told her, capturing her lips once again.

Nineteen

"I can't believe the hearing is tomorrow," Charlotte said, propping her feet up and rubbing her swollen belly. "Lily will be officially ours." Holding the phone between her ear and her shoulder, she smiled as she watched Lily playing on the floor with her set of colorful blocks.

Already three months had passed since Anthony had begged her to help. And now here they were, on the road to a happier marriage with two babies.

"I can't leave New York until tomorrow morning, so I'll have to meet you at the courthouse," Anthony told her. "I have a meeting with Bronson and a couple of the actors and their agents before I can leave. We're just finalizing everything. Looks like the project is going just as we all hoped. Olivia is really anxious to get started."

Charlotte swallowed the niggling of fear that crept up at this turn in the conversation: he was talking movies and not about gaining permanent guardianship of his niece tomorrow.

"I felt the baby move today," she told him. "At least I think that's what it was. The feeling was the same as the description in my pregnancy books."

"That's great, Charlie. Listen, I need to run. We're on our way out the door for dinner. I'll meet you at the courthouse tomorrow. Love you, babe."

And then he was gone.

Charlotte stared at the handset, unsure of what to think. She knew he was excited about this film, the one he'd waited for for so long. But at the same time, they'd gone to a few therapy sessions, they'd had a breakthrough in Tahoe and the night of the Children's Hospital wing dedication, and she'd thought they were really on the right path.

But in the week he'd been in New York, he'd only called twice to check in. In his defense, she knew he'd be busy. This was the biggest film he or Bronson had ever done, and because it was depicting their mother, they were pulling out all the stops to make this the greatest production.

Lily let out a squeal and knocked over her blocks, clapping at the colorful mess she'd created.

Charlotte joined Lily on the floor and started the rebuilding game so Lily could knock them down again.

"I feel like you're ours already," she told Lily. "Tomorrow it's official. You're going to be the best big sister."

Lily stared up at her, chewing on a red block, drool covering her fingers as she sucked.

"I think you're getting some teeth."

Charlotte tried to concentrate on the blocks, on the fact that in less than twenty-four hours Lily would be theirs legally, and that in five months they would welcome another baby.

But it was impossible to block out the worry that had settled in. She only hoped that when Anthony returned home tomorrow, they would continue this upward climb together.

For the past few months they'd grown stronger together and had constructed a firmer foundation for their marriage. The stability she'd been missing for most of her life had been slowly worked in, and Anthony was definitely the reason. He'd been so attentive, so eager to meet the needs of "his girls," as he called them. She'd seen him ask his assistant to take more control over his emails and phone calls so he could concentrate more on family life.

But now that he was back into project mode, would this last?

She would be able to tell tomorrow when she saw him at the courthouse. She hated they couldn't arrive together, but they would enter the courtroom together, putting up a united front for Lily.

"That's right." She leaned over and kissed Lily on the head. "Uncle Anthony and I are going to be there for you, Lily Bug. No matter what."

"What the hell do you mean we have to reroute?"

Anthony knew that if his pilot rerouted around the storm that had settled over much of the Midwest, he'd never make it to the hearing in time.

Rerouting wasn't even an option as far as he was concerned.

"Sir, I tried to explain when we were leaving New York that there was a terrible windstorm right in our flight path."

Dammit. Anthony slapped his seat and rose to pace the luxury cabin. Yes, his pilot had told him they needed to reroute initially, but Anthony had forced him to fly on the scheduled route.

"Can we keep going and get above the storm?" Anthony asked, hopeful.

No way could he miss this court hearing. This had to be done together, not for legal reasons, but for the principle. He and Charlotte needed to be united for Lily and he wanted to be there for this monumental day in their family life. The day Lily became legally and officially theirs. He'd promised Charlotte he wouldn't let work keep him from this hearing, and he couldn't let her down. Not when they were finally in a good place again.

"I can try to keep on course, sir," his pilot said from the entry to the cockpit. "But you'll need to stay seated and fasten your seat belt. It could get bumpy and I can't make any guarantees."

Anthony nodded. "Do what you can."

He didn't want to risk their safety, but, if at all possible, he wanted them to keep going. Mother Nature was fickle and she changed so often. This storm could vanish or move in another direction.

Anthony had known about the unfavorable weather before takeoff, but he hadn't called Charlotte to tell her about a possible delay for two reasons: one, it was so early in L.A. when he'd departed that he didn't want to wake her, and, two, he didn't want to unnecessarily upset her if he could indeed arrive on time.

He took his seat once again, tightening his belt and praying they would arrive safely and on time in L.A. He had to make that court hearing. Years of letdowns had nearly murdered their marriage. How would she react if he wasn't there by her side on one of the most important days of their life?

"The judge is ready for you in his chambers, Mrs. Price."

Charlotte glanced toward the doorway once again, and once again it was still empty. Anthony wasn't showing.

A sick feeling came over her. He'd gotten caught up with his career. The old Charlotte wouldn't have been surprised, but the new Charlotte—the one who'd given the new Anthony the benefit of the doubt—was shocked. She hated herself for placing so much stock in how well he seemed to be adjusting to being the perfect family man. More than likely he'd lost track of time with his morning meeting and had taken off late…that is, if he'd left at all.

He hadn't even called her cell to tell her, and when she'd tried to reach him, it had gone straight to voice mail.

"Mrs. Price?" the clerk called again. "If you're ready."

Charlotte pasted on a smile, shifted Lily on her hip and shouldered the diaper bag. "Yes, we're ready."

This was not at all how she'd pictured this day going. As Charlotte entered the judge's chambers, she couldn't believe she was doing this alone. They'd come so far to have this backslide.

But right now she would not feel sorry for herself that once again she was being pushed aside for business. She would concentrate on Lily—this sweet, precious bundle who needed a good life, a good, stable home. And Charlotte vowed, no matter what, she would provide that.

In no time at all, the judge declared Lily legally the dependent of Anthony and Charlotte. For such a monumental moment, it was simple and quick.

Charlotte had originally had images of the three of them going out for a celebratory lunch.

"Looks like it's just me and you," she told Lily as she descended the courthouse steps. She only hoped that wouldn't be the mantra for the rest of Lily's life.

Charlotte wasn't in much of a mood to go out for lunch, so she decided to just head home and put Lily down for her afternoon nap. Maybe Anthony would show up at the house later…maybe not.

Once she strapped Lily in her car seat, Charlotte checked her phone once again for missed calls. Nothing. Not even a text.

Resisting the urge to throw the phone and kick her tires, she slid behind the wheel and counted to ten. Then she counted backward. But it was when she looked into the mirror and saw a smiling, happy child that she realized that she had to be strong. There was a baby depending on her, and another baby who would soon need her strength, too.

"I will not let myself get worked up again," she whispered as she started the car. "I've known all along that this could happen."

She just hated that stupid saying that kept playing in her head. *Fool me once, shame on you. Fool me twice, shame on me.*

* * *

Anthony didn't even bother with his luggage in the car. He didn't care about anything but getting inside to see Charlotte and Lily. God, he was sick just thinking of everything that had likely raced through her head in the hours since they were scheduled to meet at the courthouse.

Once his plane had finally landed in L.A., he'd tried calling her cell, only to get voice mail. More than likely she'd looked right at the screen and thrown the phone across the room.

But if she only knew what he'd gone through to get back to her, she'd know the circumstances were beyond his control.

Damn Mother Nature and lack of cell towers in no-name cornfields in whatever the hell state his plane had had to make an emergency landing.

Anthony burst through the front door and immediately went up the stairs toward the nursery. Charlotte was probably giving Lily her nighttime bath.

Sure enough, at the top of the stairs he heard squeals coming from the bath. His heart clenched. This is what he would be coming home to every day. How could he not count his blessings? Laughter, love, happiness.

If he could just convince Charlotte that he had a legitimate reason for being late—six hours late to be exact—they could have it all.

But would she understand? Granted, Mother Nature had certainly caused the delay, but at the same time, if he hadn't been away on business, he would've been at that court hearing with no problem.

He made enough noise in the hall to alert her to his presence. He didn't want to add fear on top of what was sure to be anger.

As he rounded the corner of the bath, he smiled when he saw Charlotte wrap Lily in a pink hooded princess towel with the hood as a big terry-cloth tiara.

She turned, looked straight into his eyes and without a word, went back to towel-drying Lily.

"I'm sorry," he said, not bothering with excuses. "I know you're sick of those words, but it couldn't be helped."

Charlotte picked up a towel-wrapped Lily and nudged past him. "Also words I'm tired of hearing."

Well, at least she was speaking to him. He feared he'd come home to complete silence. He followed her into the nursery and leaned against the doorjamb.

"I'm getting her ready for bed," Charlotte said without turning to look at him. "I'm also not going to argue in front of her. If you have something to say, it can wait."

Anthony didn't move, didn't say a word, he merely stood in the doorway watching what had become the nightly ritual of putting lotion on Lily's porcelain skin and sliding her into a soft sleeper.

"I'll go make the bottle," he offered.

Charlotte zipped up the pajamas. "I already made it and brought it up before the bath."

Picking up the baby and kissing her on the nose, Charlotte moved across the room, flicked on the soft, soothing lullaby and picked up the bottle from the cribside table. Anthony thought he'd watch her rock Lily to sleep and enjoy listening to her hum along with the gentle music, but instead Charlotte moved to the door and slowly closed it, forcing him to back out into the hall.

Okay. Better than a slap in the face and nothing less than he deserved.

Because he knew she'd be a while, probably out of spite more than how long it took for Lily to fall asleep, he went downstairs and retrieved his bags from the car.

After he put the bags in their bedroom, he went to grab a shower. He'd been traveling all day and had been stuck in some godforsaken field in Kansas or wherever the hell it was. He'd opted to wait out the storm by checking every fifteen seconds for a cell signal. He should've been smart enough to stay behind like Bronson and wait out the bad weather.

Frustrated, angry and more than worried that Charlotte wouldn't understand, Anthony hurried through his shower and was just stepping back into the bedroom fisting a towel in his hand when Charlotte came in.

"I hope you don't think that's going to distract me," she told him, her eyes raking down to his bare chest then back up.

"No, I thought you'd take longer," he answered honestly. "How was the court hearing?"

"The one you missed earlier today?" she asked with a sweet smile on her face. "Oh, it was lonely, embarrassing, and I had to make up excuses as to why one of the guardians couldn't make it. Simply saying you were too selfish wouldn't have looked good, so I explained that you were out of town on business. I even painted lies all around you by saying how you're the poster child for a family man and that you're devoted to your work so we can have all the nice things that Lily will need as well as loving people who adore her."

Still clutching his towel, Anthony remained rooted to the plush carpet. "I'm sorry you felt you had to lie for me. I'm even more sorry you were alone and embarrassed."

With one hand on her swollen belly, Charlotte swiped away a tear with the other hand. "Being sorry is the story of our marriage, Anthony. You don't know how I thought you'd changed, how I'd hoped and prayed. Before you left on this trip, I worried once you started this filming cycle again, that your niece and your pregnant wife would be brushed aside for the new and exciting. And I was right."

He took a step forward. "Charlie—"

"No," she said, holding up a hand. "Don't say another word. I had a terrible feeling you'd push me to the bottom of the list, but to do it to two innocent children is intolerable."

Fear, dread and just plain guilt squeezed his chest. "I did everything I could to get back here."

"Really?" Sarcasm dripped from her voice as she moved over to the bed and sat on the edge. Lacing her hands around her slightly swollen stomach, she added, "And was this before or after you spent the day with A-list actors, their agents and your brother?"

"After," he said through gritted teeth. "I left on time, as I told you I was going to. Please, hear me out before deciding that I'm the scum of the earth and not worthy."

Without a word, she merely quirked a brow.

"Before we took off, my pilot warned me we should reroute due to a windstorm over the Midwest. I refused and told him to go ahead and stay on course." Anthony crossed to the bed, propped one hand on the thick post and looked down at his beautiful, he hoped forgiving, wife. "I didn't call because it was early here and I truly didn't think there would be a problem. As we drew closer, the pilot was told there was no way he could fly through and we needed to reroute. But before he could, we were forced to make an emergency landing in some field in Kansas."

"Anthony, this story—"

"Is the truth," he told her. "I'm good, but I'm not this good. We had to wait out the storm in the plane and I swear it felt like we were rocking back and forth. There was no way we could've taken off. There was no cell service. I tried stepping off the plane, I tried walking to different ends of the plane, but nothing. We were honest-to-God in the middle of nowhere and there was no way to contact you."

Anthony stopped, waited for her to say something, but silence filled the room and he knew he'd taken one giant leap backward and had landed right where he had started three months ago.

"I know this sounds ridiculous," he went on. "But I tried to get back in time. I tried."

Charlotte looked down at her stomach, rubbed the swell before looking back up at him, tears shimmering in her bright green eyes. "And what will happen when you're gone and you try to get back for the birth of our baby? What will happen if

I go into labor early or something goes wrong? Will you miss everything but expect my immediate forgiveness because you tried?"

"I wouldn't miss the birth of our child," he told her, hating this position he'd put them in again.

"You didn't think you'd miss the court date to gain legal custody of Lily, though, did you?"

Anthony sighed, moving over to sit on the bed next to Charlotte. "No, I didn't, but I won't put myself in that position again where I'm cutting things too close."

Charlotte came to her feet, looked down at him and nodded. "You're right. You won't."

A sick feeling of dread overcame him.

"Charlie," he said, reaching for her, but she stepped back and lifted her chin.

"I love you, Anthony, but I have to love myself and love these babies enough to know when we deserve better than leftovers." She moved to the dresser where she pulled out a pair of pajamas. "I'll be in the guest room on the other side of Lily. Tomorrow I will work on finding a place of my own."

"You can't mean this," he pleaded. "You can't give up when we've come so far."

Charlotte turned, clutching her clothing to her chest. "I never gave up. Don't you see, Anthony? It was you all along. You tried, but in the end everything still hinged on your career—not the future of your niece and our marriage, not to mention this baby I'm carrying. So don't tell me not to give up when I've tried for years to show you my love. I just can't make you love me enough, and I deserve better."

Anthony let her walk from the room. He'd stressed her enough and she needed to be alone. So did he, because she was right. She did deserve better, and who was he to just expect her to wait around for him to realize it?

Still clad in only his towel, Anthony lay back on the king-sized bed and stared up at the peaked canopy. The issue wasn't that he was late because of plane problems. The issue was that he'd cut his career and his personal life so close together that he'd inadvertently made the decision as to which one was more important.

He ran a hand over his face and resisted the urge to scream and curse. What good would it do? Who would he yell at? There was no one to blame here but himself. There was nothing he could do tonight to make Charlotte understand that he truly loved her, loved these babies and loved this marriage. He'd explained what had happened, but she hadn't cared. He couldn't blame her.

But he could start, right now, by making this right. The move was risky, and he might end up losing everything he'd ever wanted, but he had to try. He had to make her see that she was the number-one priority in his life. Charlotte and the babies were his life, and he couldn't just give up now. Not when they'd come so far and so much was at stake.

Twenty

Charlotte rang the doorbell of her Hollywood Hills home. Nerves settled in her stomach as she stood there waiting for the door to open.

A week ago she'd left and had gone to stay with her friend until she could find a place of her own. She'd been by to see Lily almost every day, but she'd only stayed a little while because being back in the house, knowing what she could never have, rubbed that raw spot on her heart.

But this morning when she'd gotten on her laptop to check a few new places that had gone on the market, one of the main headlines had captured her attention, stolen her breath and changed her life.

So here she was, ready to see what was going on, to see if what she'd read was true, and if so, to beg for another chance.

The door swung open and Monique stood there with a stunned expression on her face. "Mrs. Price, I don't know why you insist on ringing the bell."

Charlotte returned the smile and stepped over the threshold. "Because this is Anthony's house now, Monique. Is he around?"

"It's your house, too," the maid mumbled as she turned in the foyer. "He's in the Florida room with Lily."

Charlotte moved through the house and found Anthony crawling on his hands and knees around a big potted plant. She stood in the doorway and smiled.

"What are you looking for?" she asked.

Anthony jerked his head up. "I'm chasing Lily Bug around."

Just then Lily walked around the sofa and giggled before falling on her diapered butt.

"Oh, my gosh," Charlotte squealed. "She wasn't walking yesterday when I saw her."

Anthony came to his feet. "She was really trying last night and this morning she kind of took off. She's been going all around, especially if she's holding something."

Charlotte didn't want to tear up over missing Lily's first major milestone, but dammit, these pregnancy hormones were out of control.

"I can't believe I missed it," Charlotte said, picking up Lily and giving her kisses on her nose. "You're going to be into everything now. Yes, you are."

Anthony came to his feet and kicked some wayward blocks out of the way. "I'll let you visit with her."

When he started to walk out, Charlotte called his name. "Don't go. I actually came to talk to you."

He placed his hands on his hips and it was then that Charlotte noticed Mr. Hotshot Director who wore Armani like a second skin now resembled Mr. Mom. With his disheveled hair, baby-food stains on his gray T-shirt and no shoes, he could so play the roll of stay-at-home mom.

"Is it about the baby?" he asked. "I still want to come to all the appointments."

Charlotte gently placed Lily back on the floor to continue

playing. "No, I'm not here about the baby. I'm here to see if it's true."

He studied her face, the muscle ticking in his jaw. "Yes."

Charlotte wasn't surprised he knew exactly what she was asking. "Why?" she asked.

He shrugged and crossed the room to take a seat on the plush white sofa. "I needed to make a choice between my family and my career. I made it. It's not as if I need to work to support myself."

Charlotte stared at him, unable to believe what she was hearing. "You quit the one project you'd been dying to get so you could take care of your family?"

"I may have lost you over my decisions, but I still need to make sure I'm there for the kids." His eyes drifted out onto the pool, and that muscle ticked in his jaw again. "I won't have them doubt my love."

A piece of Charlotte's heart broke at his soft words. He was trying to be the perfect father and she'd totally ignored that he wasn't going to be perfect and this was who he was. She'd fallen in love with the man—director and all.

She moved on into the room and stood next to his chair until he looked up at her.

"They never would've doubted your love," she told him. "And I was a fool to think you hadn't changed."

"No," he corrected before she could speak further. "Had I not cut my trip so close, I would've been there for the court date. I would've made my commitment to our family, but I wasn't there because I was too busy trying to fit in everything in a short amount of time. I won't do that to you or the kids anymore. Ever."

Charlotte squatted down beside him, laying her hand on his knee. "I came by to talk some sense into you. I wanted you to know that I can see how much you value this family and I know you're living your own hell inside by beating yourself up over what happened."

He didn't speak, but his eyes slid to Lily as she played with her baby doll and bottle. His lips thinned, a sure sign that he was upset.

"Listen." She squeezed his leg until his focus came back to her. "I think we both went into this ninety-day period with the wrong attitude. I thought it could produce a miracle and you thought you could be the perfect husband, father and director. But we both messed up. We both need to own up to our mistakes and just realize we're human and we're going to screw up."

Anthony reached out and cupped the side of her face. "Damn, Charlotte. You have no idea how much I want to be the perfect everything for you. I never want to let you down, but I find myself doing it over and over."

"And I keep throwing it in your face," she added. "If you weren't willing to love me and these babies the way we need, you never would've given up the film. Please, Anthony. Don't lose a piece of yourself by trying to prove something. Call Bronson and tell him you made a mistake."

He surged to his feet, raking a hand through his hair. "You don't get it. I don't care about the film, Charlie. I want you back. I left the project because I wanted to focus on us. Even though you swore we were through, I knew if I just left completely and focused on the children, you'd come around and we could...I don't know. Start over."

Warmth, love and hope spread through her.

"You quit to focus on being a father?" she asked.

"I didn't know any other way to get your attention and prove to you how sorry I am than to put my sole focus on the children...and hopefully, you."

Charlotte's heart broke at the sacrifice he'd made, but she also couldn't help but think that maybe she'd pushed him too far.

Closing the gap between them, she placed her hands on the sides of his face. "I want you to call Bronson and tell him you want back in. Then I want you to go to my car and get my suitcase because I'm coming back home."

His hands slid over her baby bump as a smile spread across his face. "Are you sure? Can we really do this?"

"I want you to do what you love," she told him. "I don't want you to do what I want you to do. You can't live your life just for me."

"Oh, Charlie," he whispered, kissing her lips softly. "I can live my life for you and these babies. I'll do whatever I can to keep all of you happy."

"Then get back in this project and keep this film in the family."

He kissed her again. "Because family is everything."

Epilogue

Anthony had tripped over dolls, spilled a sippy cup of apple juice down the front of his shirt and gone through all the wipes in the diaper bag when Lily had had her major explosion in her diaper.

But he wouldn't trade these moments for anything, even if they were all taking place on the set of the upcoming film.

He sat down in his director's chair and watched her play at his feet.

It wouldn't be long before his own little girl arrived.

"Sorry I'm late." Charlotte breezed in and stepped over the cords running along the concrete floor. "I tried to leave, but Hannah loves to talk."

"I take it the interior designing went well, then?" he asked, coming to his feet to kiss her cheek.

"Beautifully." Charlotte beamed. "She's starting immediately in the guest room on the other side of Lily's and she had some great ideas."

Anthony bent down to pick up Lily. "We've had a great time learning all about the set of movies."

With a laugh, Charlotte ran a finger over his damp, stained shirt. "I see that. Was she too much trouble? I really wouldn't have minded taking her with me."

"She was fine," he assured. "I'm thrilled I can bring her here. Movies will be in her blood. Who knows? She may be directing our lives when we're older."

Charlotte rubbed her protruding belly and he couldn't help but smile. How lucky was he not only to be given a second chance but to have two children to complete his family?

"So she's going to direct biographies?" Charlotte asked with a sly grin.

Anthony wrapped an arm around her waist and hugged her to his side. "More like romance."

"I love you, Anthony."

"I know you do." He kissed her forehead as he held Lily on his hip. "I love you more each day."

"Would you like to show me around?" she asked.

Anthony stepped back. "Seriously?"

"Why not? I've never visited your set before. I'd like to be part of this. You took so much interest in my volunteer work. I think it's important for us to support each other."

The therapist had agreed, too.

"I'd love to show you this side of my life." He took her hand and led her through. "Watch the cords."

Just then she tripped. Lightning-fast reflexes had him wrapping an arm around her to support her while keeping Lily on his other side.

"My balance is a bit off with this extra weight in the front," she joked. "Thanks for catching me."

"Always, Charlie." He gazed into her eyes and smiled. "I'll always be here to catch you."

* * * * *

REQUEST YOUR FREE BOOKS!
2 FREE NOVELS PLUS 2 FREE GIFTS!

Harlequin® *Desire*

ALWAYS POWERFUL, PASSIONATE AND PROVOCATIVE

YES! Please send me 2 FREE Harlequin Desire® novels and my 2 FREE gifts (gifts are worth about $10). After receiving them, if I don't wish to receive any more books, I can return the shipping statement marked "cancel." If I don't cancel, I will receive 6 brand-new novels every month and be billed just $4.30 per book in the U.S. or $4.99 per book in Canada. That's a saving of at least 14% off the cover price! It's quite a bargain! Shipping and handling is just 50¢ per book in the U.S. and 75¢ per book in Canada.* I understand that accepting the 2 free books and gifts places me under no obligation to buy anything. I can always return a shipment and cancel at any time. Even if I never buy another book, the two free books and gifts are mine to keep forever.

225/326 HDN FEF3

Name	(PLEASE PRINT)	
Address		Apt. #
City	State/Prov.	Zip/Postal Code

Signature (if under 18, a parent or guardian must sign)

Mail to the **Reader Service:**
IN U.S.A.: P.O. Box 1867, Buffalo, NY 14240-1867
IN CANADA: P.O. Box 609, Fort Erie, Ontario L2A 5X3

Not valid for current subscribers to Harlequin Desire books.

Want to try two free books from another line?
Call 1-800-873-8635 or visit www.ReaderService.com.

* Terms and prices subject to change without notice. Prices do not include applicable taxes. Sales tax applicable in N.Y. Canadian residents will be charged applicable taxes. Offer not valid in Quebec. This offer is limited to one order per household. All orders subject to credit approval. Credit or debit balances in a customer's account(s) may be offset by any other outstanding balance owed by or to the customer. Please allow 4 to 6 weeks for delivery. Offer available while quantities last.

Your Privacy—The Reader Service is committed to protecting your privacy. Our Privacy Policy is available online at www.ReaderService.com or upon request from the Reader Service.

We make a portion of our mailing list available to reputable third parties that offer products we believe may interest you. If you prefer that we not exchange your name with third parties, or if you wish to clarify or modify your communication preferences, please visit us at www.ReaderService.com/consumerschoice or write to us at Reader Service Preference Service, P.O. Box 9062, Buffalo, NY 14269. Include your complete name and address.

HDES11B

New York Times *bestselling author Brenda Jackson*
presents TEXAS WILD,
a brand-new Westmoreland novel.

Available October 2012 from Harlequin Desire®!

Rico figured there were a lot of things in life he didn't
know. But the one thing he did know was that there was no
way Megan Westmoreland was going to Texas with him.
He was attracted to her, big-time, and had been from the
moment he'd seen her at Micah's wedding four months ago.
Being alone with her in her office was bad enough. But
the idea of them sitting together on a plane or in a car was
arousing him just thinking about it.

He could tell by the mutinous expression on her face that
he was in for a fight. That didn't bother him. Growing up,
he'd had two younger sisters to deal with, so he knew well
how to handle a stubborn female.

She crossed her arms over her chest. "Other than the fact
that you prefer working alone, give me another reason I
can't go with you."

He crossed his arms over his own chest. "I don't need
another reason. You and I talked before I took this case, and
I told you I would get you the information you wanted…
doing things my way."

He watched as she nibbled on her bottom lip. So now she
was remembering. Good. Even so, he couldn't stop looking
into her beautiful dark eyes, meeting her fiery gaze head-on.

"As the client, I demand that you take me," she said.

He narrowed his gaze. "You can demand all you want,
but you're not going to Texas with me."

Megan's jaw dropped. "I *will* be going with you since there's no good reason that I shouldn't."

He didn't say anything for a moment. "Okay, there is another reason I won't take you with me. One that you'd do well to consider," he said in a barely controlled tone. She had pushed him, and he didn't like being pushed.

"Fine, let's hear it," she snapped furiously.

He placed his hands in the pockets of his jeans, stood with his legs braced apart and leveled his gaze on her. "I want you, Megan. Bad. And if you go anywhere with me, I'm going to have you."

He then turned and walked out of her office.

Will Megan go to Texas with Rico?

Find out in Brenda Jackson's brand-new Westmoreland novel, TEXAS WILD.

Available October 2012 from Harlequin Desire®.

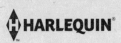

n o c t u r n e™

Satisfy your paranormal cravings with two dark
and sensual new werewolf tales from
Harlequin® Nocturne™!

FOREVER WEREWOLF
by Michele Hauf

Can sexy, charismatic werewolf Trystan Hawkes win the
heart of Alpine pack princess Lexi Connors—or will dark
family secrets cost him the pack's trust…and her love?

THE WOLF PRINCESS
by Karen Whiddon

Will Dr. Braden Streib risk his life to save royal wolf shifter
Princess Alisa—even if it binds them inescapably together
in a battle against a deadly faction?

**Plus look for a reader-favorite story
included in each book!**

2 GREAT NOVELS

SAME GREAT PRICE

Available September 18, 2012